NIGHT OF SWORD AND SHIELD

SONG OF THE FALLEN SWORDS
BOOK 2

RYAN KIRK

WATERSTONE
MEDIA

For Joy,
My constant guide through the world of education

PROLOGUE

Kaya woke from her nightmare with a start, the shadows that had chased her through her dreams creeping into the darkest corners of her tiny bedroom. The room was already as dark as a tomb, but the shadow that pursued her was darker yet. Though she was under a half dozen thick, woolen blankets, she shivered as she sensed the darkness surrounding her.

She sealed her lips shut against the urge to whimper. To cry out was to invite reprimand or, worse, sympathy that was thinner than a sheet of worn paper. The only presence in her room less welcome than the darkness was that of her parents and their loud, empty proclamations of love. She pulled the blankets up to her chin and wiggled deeper as though her bed was capable of providing the comfort her parents didn't.

The darkness surrounded, but it didn't touch. There were nights when Kaya wished it would. Its silent promises of violence and sacrifice were somehow worse than the deeds themselves. She preferred the sting of her cheek to the threat of an upraised hand. The sting might hurt, but it meant the pain was over and the healing could begin.

In defiance of the suffocating shadows, she closed her eyes and sought the Song. It was warmth and light, always present, always hidden just beneath the surface of things. Its melodies were of love and meaning, of right action and a deeper order. The Master might never use such language to describe the music, but every passing year added another layer of doubt on top of her childhood beliefs.

By her counting, she was twelve, and though no one celebrated the day of her birth anymore, she was certain her thirteenth approached soon. That day, which was supposed to be a celebration, now scared her. She couldn't point to any one detail and justify her fear, but she sensed the danger of it, like a prey animal being hunted by one of the beasts of the surface.

It was in the quiet whispers her parents shared after they thought she was sound asleep. In the way the Master tested her more regularly now, as though afraid she wouldn't be ready to perform for an important event. More than anything, it was in the way the darkness hung over her bed at night, patiently but eagerly awaiting a day that quickly approached.

She listened to the Song and took comfort in its reassurances. The world she walked was wrong and twisted, but the world beyond her invisible cage still listened to the pure Song, the notes that the darkness hadn't corrupted.

She hoped that someday she'd experience that world.

As she sank deeper into the Song, its notes changed. They took on an edge, a sharpness that hadn't been there before. She focused, listening to the Song with both body and spirit.

The Song didn't sing itself in words, but with concepts, with the base reality of the world, that language could only point at. It couldn't be translated but only understood. Tonight, the Song called for her in a way it never had before. It pleaded for her and showed her what must be done. Her eyes went wide as she understood.

Despite everything she endured daily, the greater part of her resisted. Such was the comfort of the familiar, even if the familiar was cold, heartless, and full of lies. It was still the world she knew, and the Song asked for her to give up all of it.

She trusted the Song. It was the only part of her life that was true and good, but it had never asked so much from her.

The darkness surged around her as though it knew what transpired in the secret chambers of Kaya's heart. She was sure it intended to intimidate, but it convinced her instead. Even if the Song demanded everything of her, it would take less than those who glued empty smiles upon their faces and claimed they loved her.

She threw her covers off, rolled out of bed, and got dressed in the pitch darkness of her room. Her parents were still awake and in the living room, and they'd react as soon as they saw a light under her door. Better for her to take the lead while she could.

Once dressed, she cast her imagination around the room, wondering if there was anything else she should take. There was precious little for her to consider. It had been years since her parents had seen fit to gift her with a toy, claiming they were too childish for someone as important as her. Everything that was precious was hidden in her memories, so there was nothing to take.

She turned to face the door and took a steadying breath. As soon as her heart stopped pounding in her chest, she reached out and switched on the light. The lone lamp on the wall came to life, filling her room with a soft, warm light gifted to her from the Engine.

As she expected, the light's appearance caused a quiet commotion in the living room as her parents untangled themselves from one another on the couch. She opened the door and stepped through before they could finish straightening their clothes. Light from her room spilled out into the living room, and she advanced, staying within the warm glow.

"Is something wrong, Kaya?" Father asked, trying to sound solemn even though he hadn't yet gotten his pants up past his knees.

"Yes, Kaya, is something wrong?" Mother echoed. She was more annoyed than concerned, but Kaya thought she saw something else in her eyes, and it was confirmed when Mother glanced away, unable to meet her daughter's even gaze.

She feared Kaya.

So did Father, but he disguised it better. "Kaya?" he asked.

She turned her gaze to him, but he didn't look away. Of the two, he was the stronger, the one who truly believed. Mother followed, content to be standing in his shadow as he strode toward his brighter future.

He was the one who would need to be convinced, but fortunately, he was the easier of the two to convince. He already believed, and so everything he saw and heard was squeezed into the box of those beliefs, making him susceptible to deception. Mother, not so strong in her husband's faith, tended to see events and people more as they were.

"The Engine speaks to me," she said. "It calls to me tonight."

Mother shook her head, but Father leaned forward, his pants forgotten for the moment. "What does it say?"

Kaya shrugged, feigning indifference. Her parents might be blinded by their beliefs and their ambition, but they weren't so blind as to miss that Kaya considered her gift equal parts blessing and curse. "That's all I can hear, but it won't let me sleep. I think I need to visit the Engine tonight."

It seemed such an apparent lie to Kaya, but Father nodded as though he'd been expecting something like this. Mother was skeptical, but she kept her thoughts to herself. Father wouldn't listen to her anyway, not now. She stood. "If you're going to take her, you should go now." She leaned in close and whispered loudly enough for Kaya to hear. "I'll keep the bed warm for you."

Kaya didn't miss the way Mother's eyes gleefully flicked over to her as she whispered into Father's ear, but she pretended to be oblivious. She made Kaya call her mother, but she wasn't the woman who'd given her life to give birth to Kaya. She'd only found Father after he'd become one of Nightkeep's Singers, and thus entitled to privileges few other families enjoyed.

Father nodded eagerly, and the decision was made without debate. He finished pulling his pants up as he stood. He considered for a moment, then threw on the white robes of his order, straightening them out in a mirror before gesturing for the two of them to leave the home.

Out in the hallway, all the lamps had been dimmed for the evening hours. Father pointed outward. "We'll take you to see the Master. He'll want to hear what you have to say."

Kaya masked the sudden pounding of her heart with a quick nod. Father led the way, though Kaya had walked this very route so often the past few weeks she was halfway convinced she could navigate the twisting passages with her eyes closed.

Two full-fledged Swords guarded the Master's door, and they didn't seem particularly pleased to have their quiet evening interrupted by a disheveled Singer and his strange daughter.

"What do you want?" the first guard growled.

Kaya stared hard at her feet, convinced that if she so much as glanced up, they would know she had lied.

Father, thankfully, was more than happy to serve as her unwitting shield. He was a Singer, used to respect and deference, and didn't take kindly to the guard's short temper. "We're here to see the Master, and before you tell me he's sleeping, I know, but this is important enough that he would want to be woken up. I'm not fool enough to risk his wrath otherwise."

There was a moment of silence, then one of the guards grunted and went inside the Master's home to wake him.

They waited, and Kaya continued to stare at her feet. The light leather shoes she wore were getting small, her big toe close to punching out of its tight confinement.

A minute later, the door opened and the guard said, "You can go into the living room. He'll be with you in a moment."

It was either a sign of their trust or due to a direct order from the Master, but the guards let the pair in without an escort. Kaya allowed herself a small sigh of relief. The first challenges had been overcome, but the most difficult remained.

"Look up," Father said quietly.

Kaya didn't want to, but it was good advice, so she did. The Master's room was a study in understated elegance. His living room was the size of Kaya's entire apartment, and it was filled with a variety of plush rocking chairs that looked like they hadn't been sat in since the day they'd entered the home. Two paintings hung on opposite walls. One was an artist's representation of the three great cities of Nightkeep, and the other was of a landscape, of a surface Kaya had never seen with her own eyes. She wondered if the placement of the paintings had any significance.

She stepped closer to the landscape painting. It called to her, not like the Song did, but it sparked something primal, a desire to stand on top of a rocky promontory and look out over the land. She belonged on the surface.

It was a fool's dream, of course. If she wanted a view,

anyone could see farther by visiting any of the observation platforms at the bottom of the city, but it wasn't the same as hiking to the top of a hill. She didn't know why she was so convinced of that fact, but her spirit sang as she imagined the breathless views from the top of a mountain peak.

The song ended the moment the Master stepped into the room, the darkness from Kaya's room and nightmares hiding comfortably in his shadow.

Kaya and Father both bowed deeply, instinct and tradition taking over. The Master grumbled, "What's the meaning of this?"

"My daughter, Master," Father said.

The Master turned to her, a question written in his gaze.

She did her best not to flinch away from that hard stare but took comfort in knowing few met his eyes directly. "As I slept tonight, the Engine called to me. It wants me to visit, though for what reason, I do not know."

The Master's eyes flicked to her wrists. "Were you in contact with any shards?"

Kaya cast her eyes down. "No, Master."

It was dangerous to admit as much. They believed the Song could only be heard through the shards, but their imaginations were limited by ancient traditions. Admitting she could hear the Song without made her even more important in their eyes. It meant her scheme might work, but it also meant they would never willingly let her go.

He thought for a moment. The darkness hiding in his shadow roiled, eager to escape its bounds and wrap itself around her. For now, the Song kept it at bay. Kaya waited for her answer, almost certain it would be "no."

"Then let's see what we can learn," the Master said. He looked at Father. "It's earlier than I expected, but we'd be fools not to seize the opportunity. Even if it's nothing, it's worth the loss of a few hours of sleep."

Father nodded. "I'd thought the same."

They left the Master's home together, the Master on her right and Father on her left. The two guards, always by the Master's side, followed half a dozen paces behind. Darkness surrounded her, shifting as the adults' shadows twisted when they walked past the dimly lit hallway lamps. It cackled as though laughing at her plan. She couldn't hear the Song over its mocking, but she hoped she wouldn't be cut off for long.

Every door opened to the Master without question on their journey inward and toward the Engine room. As they reached a stairwell and started down the steep and narrow passage, Master asked, "What did it feel like?"

She'd feared a questioning like this. The Master believed in the darkness, just as Father did, but he justified his beliefs with the veneer of reason. He was more likely to find holes in her explanations.

"It was like a tug on my spirit. A sensation that I had to go to the Engine room immediately."

"I'm eager to learn what's in store for you," Master said.

The tone of his voice made her shiver, and she suddenly doubted the wisdom of trusting the Song. The Master's eagerness was palpable, and hadn't he said, back in his home, that it was earlier than he'd expected?

What if she'd fallen under the influence of the darkness, too? She felt certain it was the Song, but could she know for sure? If the shadow could sway skilled men like Father and Master, what hope did she have against it?

Unfortunately, the time for doubt had ended when she'd turned the light on in her room. Since that moment, her path had been determined. All that remained was to see where the path led.

The closer they came to the Engine, the farther the darkness receded. It stopped surrounding Kaya, opting instead to hide within the shadows of Master and Father. As it condensed, she felt its power more clearly, the hooks it set deep in the hearts of the two men.

She felt sorry for Father. How much of his behavior toward her was because of the darkness and how much came from his own heart? There was no way to tell, and she wasn't sure she'd ever know.

By the time they reached the door to the Engine room, the darkness had retreated nearly all the way back into its hosts. The Master bowed to the four Swords standing guard at the door and they opened it for him without question. The heavy metal door swung open silently, revealing the flickering blue light of the Engine within.

The Song wasn't as strong as it should have been, but it was clearer here than anywhere in the city. It rang with the crystal-clear tones of a silver bell, reassuring her that all was well, even amid the darkness.

The heavy door closed behind them. The metal dampened the effect of the Engine somewhat, allowing the sensitive Swords to remain on guard duty without going mad. Only Kaya, Master, and Father remained.

The Engine room was a marvel. The walls were perfectly spherical, the unfathomably powerful Engine hung from a mess of wires and cables that disappeared into the very top of the room. A metal catwalk ran around the perimeter of the room, and three balconies, evenly spaced, extended almost to the Engine itself.

The power of the Song was overwhelming, but Kaya had the training and experience necessary to hold onto her senses. She took a few steps on the catwalk, guided by the Song toward the first balcony.

The Master's firm hand came down on her shoulder, and for a moment, she feared that he, too, had heard the Song and knew what she intended. Previous experience told her it should be impossible, but she'd be a fool to underestimate the Master's skill. She forced herself to turn and give him a questioning look.

"Has it resolved into something more yet?" he asked.

She almost flinched away from the naked greed in his eyes. She didn't know what he wanted from her, didn't know what the shadow expected her to become. Whatever it was, her spirit rebelled against it. She wanted the Song and nothing more. It had been enough for Singers for generations, so what had changed to make it mean so little now?

She shook her head, and the fire in his eyes dampened a bit. "Be careful. We can't have anything happening to you."

She nodded, then pulled gently away. He let her go, following several paces behind. He didn't seem worried, but why should he? Master was the strongest Singer in two generations, and he was in a locked room protected by a half-dozen of Nightkeep's strongest Swords. If any man should feel confident, it should be him.

Kaya reached the first balcony and walked out on it, getting ever closer to the Engine. Another few steps were all she needed.

"That's close enough," Master said.

She stopped, half because obedience had long been trained into her and half because she hesitated. The temptation of the familiar remained. She could claim it had been a misunderstanding. Return to her room, the waiting darkness, and empty smiles. Her life would continue, terrible but familiar.

She hated that she even considered the possibility. It made her feel weak and a coward.

"What do you sense?" Master asked.

Should she say something? Was there anything she wanted Father to know before she left?

She couldn't think of anything. She wasn't even sure if she mattered to him anymore or if she was only a channel for his beliefs.

Kaya took two quick steps forward and reached out for the Engine. Behind her, Master realized she intended to touch the glowing stone and hurried to pull her back. No single individual could touch the stone and live, not even Master.

She touched the stone, and her world went white as she disappeared.

1

———

Radyn exited the stairwell and stepped into the bright light of the new day. He shielded his eyes from the sun's brightness and looked out over the fields. The harvest was in full swing and would hopefully be finished within the week. Groups of farmers walked their fields, cutting, pulling, and carrying their produce and grains to the ramps that would carry them to the kitchens below.

A sharp grunt and a hulking shadow from Radyn's immediate left pulled his attention away from the scene and to the young Dagger standing guard at the stairwell. Radyn didn't recognize him but wasn't too surprised. Word among the farmers was that Jyn had reduced the standards for admission into the clan and doubled their recruiting efforts.

The situation reminded Radyn of the conversation he'd had with his father the day he was killed. Father had argued the clan could only grow so large so fast if they wanted to ensure the quality of their warriors. Selection and training took time. Competence couldn't be rushed.

Jyn, the 13th Blade of Firestone, was many things, but he wasn't a fool. He'd no doubt considered every thought Radyn debated and still decided the rushed recruitment was needed. Radyn wondered what Jyn knew that he didn't.

For now, it didn't matter. Radyn was stuck dealing with a young Dagger who had all the swagger of a youthful warrior who believed they were in charge.

"What do you think you're doing here?" the Dagger sneered.

Radyn pointed out to a small plot of land, currently unoccupied except for the overflowing harvest. His plants had come in well this year. "I'm a farmer. That's the land I'm supposed to harvest today."

The Dagger's sneer remained. "Only thing you should be doing in those fields is rotting in them."

Radyn nodded. "Wait long enough and I'm sure you'll get your wish."

He watched the Dagger's hand wander close to the hilt of his maniblade. Radyn desperately hoped the Dagger wasn't so foolish, but he didn't put it past the young man. The Dagger saw that Radyn had noticed and his sneer turned into a cold smile. He stepped forward so that he was almost nose to nose with Radyn. His breath was warm and smelled of stale bread.

"Do you miss having one at your side? I bet you're thinking of trying to take mine, aren't you?" the guard asked.

Radyn remained perfectly still.

The Dagger pulled the hilt out and held it in front of him. Radyn had little doubt the fool had connected to all his shards. If Radyn moved an inch toward the hilt, the Dagger would activate the weapon, cut him down, and claim Radyn had tried to take the maniblade from him.

No one would believe the Dagger, but no one would care, either. Radyn's name had been crossed out in blood from the clan ranks. Any whiff of involvement with the clan carried a death sentence, and this young Dagger wasn't the first to tempt fate. The only reason one hadn't cut him down yet was because of Jyn. The Blade had made it clear he expected his Daggers and Swords to follow the letter of the law. It allowed him to live an uneasy existence among his fellow citizens.

When Radyn didn't move for a full minute, the young Dagger sighed theatrically and returned the hilt to his side. "If you've got a field to harvest, you're wasting your time bugging me. Get going, now."

Radyn forced himself to bow, then walked quickly to his fields. Better that than the young man decide he hadn't had enough excitement at Radyn's expense.

He'd left his tools near the center of his field, a common practice for farmers in the middle of harvest. It meant less time borrowing and returning the tools from the shacks, and it wasn't like there weren't enough tools to go around. They weren't where he had left them. He sighed and stretched while he stared at the ground where he'd set them down the night before.

Radyn searched the rows of his field for a minute before determining the tools weren't there. He walked toward the nearest shack to check out a new set. As he did, he noticed a pair of Daggers walking the fields, following him with their eyes. By itself, it didn't mean much, but their attention on him felt more focused, more intentional than usual.

At the shack, the toolmaster gave him a hard time. "There's no record of the tools being returned, either by you or by somebody else."

"I left them in my field, and someone took them."

The toolmaster's stare was hard. "You know the rules, Radyn. Everything must be returned every night. I'm happy to check you out another set, but you'll be fined for the loss of the set you borrowed yesterday unless you return them."

Radyn clenched a fist. He'd be willing to bet almost anything that not a single farmer had returned tools last night. But it wasn't worth fighting over. Not like he was trying to save up money for anything. He could imagine more than a few Shields being more than happy to arrest him for not paying his fine, too.

"Very well," he said through gritted teeth. "I'll make sure to return them every night from now on."

The toolmaster smirked. "See that you do."

Had Father ever endured this? Radyn suspected the answer was no. He'd left the clan as an honored warrior and the farmers had gladly accepted him. Radyn had thought he could follow in his father's footsteps, but the farmers didn't want him among them any more than the clan did. He was the one responsible for Nuela's death. At least, that was what everyone believed.

With new tools in hand, Radyn returned to his field and began the harvest. For a time, the troubles of the day fell from his shoulders as he bent his body to the task of harvesting Firestone's food. The sun rose high in the sky, eventually convincing Radyn to take off his shirt. His skin was darkly tanned, and his muscles were as lean as they had been when he'd been training as an initiate.

Farming didn't carry the same honor that being a Sword did, but it kept him in fighting shape.

Throughout the day, groups of farmers passed by Radyn's field, talking and laughing with one another. They carried heavy loads to the ramps that would ferry the harvest below, where it would be processed by eager teams of volunteers. A few glanced in his direction. When they did, their faces would fall, the mirth dropping from their countenances like stones dropped off the edge of the city. Then they'd look away and return to their conversations, the laughter returning to their voices.

No one was outwardly rude, but no one was kind, either.

Radyn tried to ignore the others, but their avoidance of him was like an itch he couldn't scratch. He gritted his teeth and redoubled his efforts, harvesting row after row of vegetables. When his baskets were full, he would take them to the ramps, painfully cognizant that none of the other farmers dropped off their baskets while he made the journey to and from his field.

That the frustration was familiar didn't make it any easier to forget. He kept thinking that one day, he'd come up to the fields and be perfectly content to be alone, but those moments were few and far between.

His day turned for the worse when he noticed the Daggers had increased their patrols of the surface, and no small part of their attention seemed to be directed at him. He ignored them as best he could, but they often wandered around the edges of his field like hunters scouting their prey.

By the time the bell rang for the mid-day break, Radyn had worked up a sweat and a short temper. He waited for most of the other farmers to queue, then joined near the rear, remembering to give the men and women ahead of him plenty of space. He knew himself well enough to know that if anyone wanted to pick a fight with him today, they'd get one sooner than they expected.

Thankfully, no one bothered him. He walked through the line, thanked the kitchen staff for the meal, then returned to his field to eat alone. He took his time with the meal. The Daggers were out in force, so many so that Radyn suspected something was afoot. He tamped down his curiosity before it overwhelmed him.

He wasn't part of that world anymore. No matter how he missed it. The best practice for him was to look forward. With enough effort, he could build a new life as a farmer. The others just needed more time to forget the past.

After he scraped the last of his bowl clean, he returned it to the kitchen staff and resumed his labor. Thanks to the food in his stomach and the sun on his back, he was able to shut out the rest of the world for a time.

Not long enough, though.

He heard the footsteps behind him. He didn't turn around, but a few seconds later, he heard their boots clomping haphazardly through his carefully maintained fields.

Radyn turned, more than ready to shout the Daggers down, but his frustration withered when he saw who joined them. Though Magni was twice as large as the most intimidating Dagger, he moved without so much as a whisper of fabric against the wheat. Magni's hands were loose by his side, and he kept them deliberately away from the maniblade at his hip.

Radyn bowed toward the enormous Sword. "It's been a while."

Magni grunted, and when Radyn looked into his eyes, all he saw was disgust. Rumors claimed that Magni was Jyn's most trusted guard and advisor now, but even so, Jyn hadn't shared the truth of that day with him.

Radyn wasn't sure if he was more impressed by Jyn's discretion or disappointed that even Magni would be turned against him. He'd always respected the Sword, even when Magni had kicked the daylights out of him at their first meeting. The loss of mutual respect cut deeper than any prank the farmers could pull on him.

"Not long enough," Magni said.

Radyn felt nothing but sincerity from Magni. "Why are you here?" he asked.

Magni gestured at the Daggers, who lingered behind him. They gave Radyn bitter looks, then retreated to the edge of the field to ensure the meeting remained private. No small number of farmers had turned in their direction. Some looked eager for a public execution.

"I've been receiving reports from Daggers about you. Many of them claim you're being difficult," Magni said.

Radyn's eyes narrowed. Was that really what this was about? Magni wouldn't leave Jyn's side unless there was something important demanding his attention, and Radyn doubted it was him. "No more than they give me," he answered.

Magni's eyes were cold. "From the reports I've read, it seems like you enjoy flirting with danger. More than one Dagger would have been justified in cutting you down."

"So they say. Though you may not believe it, I'm simply trying to live my life in peace."

Magni scoffed. "That would be a first." He shook his head. "But it's good that you brought up the subject of peace, because that's why I'm here."

Radyn raised a questioning eyebrow. He'd known Magni hadn't just come because of some exaggerated reports filed by the Daggers.

Magni looked around the field, making sure they weren't being listened to. Radyn wondered what could possibly be so important it would require this level of discretion. It would have been easier to tell him at home at night, but then they would have had to include Aria. Whatever was happening, they didn't want anyone else to know, not even his wife.

"Jyn has arranged a Gathering," Magni said.

"Good for him," Radyn replied.

"With Nightkeep and Starfall," Magni added.

Radyn had his hands on Magni's collar before he was even aware of his actions. He pulled the enormous man's face down to his. "What?"

The guards around the circle turned at the sudden threat. Two drew their maniblades and advanced, but

Magni held up a hand to stop them. He was so confident he hadn't even connected with his shards. He reached up and pried Radyn's hands off him with ease. Radyn didn't resist as Magni shoved him away.

The Senior Sword brushed himself off. "And you expect me to believe my Daggers wouldn't be right to take your life? I don't know what Jyn sees in you these days, but you're nothing more than a hollow shell of what you could have been if you'd learned a little discipline."

Radyn looked down so that Magni wouldn't see the storm of emotions that crossed his face. He clenched his fist but didn't say anything.

Once Radyn cooled down, Magni continued. "I don't know why I'm supposed to tell you this, but the Blade was very specific in his orders. He believes he can forge a new peace with Nightkeep, and Starfall is going to act as the witness. While that's happening behind closed doors, the citizens will enjoy the celebration."

Radyn couldn't hold back his complaints any longer. "How are we supposed to form a truce with the city that tried to sacrifice us as part of their own mad plans?"

To his surprise, Magni didn't get angry at the question. A hint of worry behind his eyes told Radyn he'd been wondering much the same. The expression only flickered in his gaze for a moment before a stoney expression replaced it. Whatever doubts Magni might hold, he wouldn't be sharing them with Radyn. Once, he might have.

"It's nothing that concerns you. The Blade has a plan, and he has assurances."

"What does he want?" Radyn could already guess the answer, but it was best if Magni confirmed it.

"He wants you to avoid the Gathering. It'll come as no surprise to you that the negotiations with Nightkeep are going to be delicate. Don't forget that whatever feelings you have for Nightkeep, they have for you, too. I hate to admit it, but between you and Nuela, you're responsible for the greatest defeats they've suffered in a generation. I wouldn't be surprised if they attempted to sneak an assassin or two on board Firestone to seek your life."

"Is Jyn providing me protection?"

Magni scoffed. "For someone whose name has been blooded by the clan? You're lucky that I'm giving you a warning. And that's all this is. The announcement will be made in the next few days, but you're not to tell anyone before then. Doing so will be considered involvement in clan affairs, is that clear?"

Radyn snorted and shook his head. If he told Aria and someone found out, they'd have all the right they wanted to kill him. "Sure. I understand."

"And once the Gathering begins, Jyn's expectation is that you do not participate, for your own safety."

"If I do, is that considered getting involved in clan affairs?"

Magni ground his teeth together. "As much as I would like to claim so, I cannot. This is Jyn's request to you. Nothing more. He doesn't want any of the trouble he's sure you're going to bring down on his head. But I can promise you, if you're the reason the peace talks with Nightkeep fail, that will definitely be considered involvement in clan affairs, and I'll personally be the one who delivers your final punishment."

Radyn gave Magni a mocking bow. "Yes, sir."

Magni's answering glare could have burned a hole straight through the core of the city. "Listen and use your head for once, Radyn. Jyn's got plans that will make life better for us all, and I'll do everything I can to make sure they come to fruition. That means keeping you out of the way. So take it from me: the best thing you can do right now is find a hole to hide in and stay there until the real warriors bring lasting peace to this city. When we're done, you can come crawling out to thank us."

2

———————

Radyn slammed the door to his apartment harder than he intended to. Aria was on the couch, reading a book about crafting the lamps and lighting fixtures that kept Firestone lit through the darkest nights. Without looking up from the book, she asked, "Rough day?"

The question was an invitation to unload all the day's burdens on her, but he hesitated. Day after day, she listened to his complaints, and though he returned the kindness, Aria complained about little. Partly, it was her disposition. After surviving the fall of Whitehawk, she'd realized that so much of what consumed other people's attention didn't matter. She endured the same number of stares and whispers as Radyn, but they bounced and slid off her like rain on a metal roof. To her mind, she had food, shelter, and someone she loved. She lacked for nothing.

Partly, though, it was because Aria's own life had blossomed in the past few months. A curious soul at heart, she'd always been interested in building and tinkering. Three months ago, she'd succeeded, after a long effort, at finding a master crafter willing to take her under her wing and indulge her curiosities.

Every morning, Aria woke up to learn more about the machines that kept the citizens of Firestone alive and comfortable. The curiosity she'd once directed toward the Engine and the shards finally found a new direction. At this point, she probably knew and understood more about Firestone than he did.

He was glad for her. He remembered well that there had been a period of a few weeks, not long after Radyn's name had been bloodied and she'd lost what little access to the shards she had, when her gloom darkened every corner of their small home. She wasn't one for dramatics. She never shouted or argued, nor did she cry or whine. Her sorrow simply pulled her spirit into shreds. She'd wandered listlessly and stared into the distance, searching for a future she'd not been sure she'd find.

Radyn had listened to what few complaints she uttered, but he'd been too wrapped up in his own forms of grief. He still felt like he hadn't done enough for her back then, but even now, Aria went out of her way to comfort and support him. He didn't deserve her, and sometimes, he feared she would realize it, too. Aria deserved nothing but the best, and he and his troubles certainly didn't qualify.

He sighed as he placed his shoes next to the wall. "Nothing new. The same complaints, another day. I'll clean up and then we can go eat."

This time, Aria looked up from her book and grinned.

That smile was enough to make his day. "Please do. I think I can smell you from here."

Radyn showered, watching the dirty water swirl around the drain and back into Firestone's water system. The water was warm but automatically turned off after two minutes, so he didn't have long. He wiped himself clean, then stepped out and dried off with a towel. By the time he emerged, he felt like a new man. "Better?"

"Much. You're home early today. Why not come over and have a seat?" Aria patted the cushion next to her.

"You make a compelling argument," Radyn said. He sat down beside her and threw his arm up so that it rested behind her head. She leaned against it and closed her eyes.

They sat for a moment in silence, and then she said, "Are you going to tell me about it?"

"Like I said, it's nothing new. When I made the agreement with Jyn, I imagined I could return to the farms, and it would be just like it had been when I was with Father. Seems foolish, now that I've had a few months to think about it. Nuela wasn't just popular among the clan. The farmers hate me just as much as the Swords and Daggers do."

Aria listened without comment. It was far from the first time their conversations had walked down these familiar paths.

"The worst part about it is that I don't think my complaint is about the farmers, though. True, farming felt more rewarding when the burden of it was shared with others, but even when I was working in the fields alone back then, I found it satisfying. Now it feels like a waste of my day."

Aria shifted so that her head was resting against his shoulder. Her hair smelled of lavender, and the scent smoothed the rough edges of his frustration. "It's been almost a year. Jyn is established now and well-liked. Perhaps he'd be willing to make a new deal. You two could tell the truth."

Radyn scoffed, and Aria tensed. "Sorry. It's very idealistic, and I wish it was possible. But if people found out Jyn's been lying to them, especially now, I don't even want to imagine how serious the consequences would be. They'd certainly turn against his peace talks with Nightkeep. He knows to keep his distance. That's why he sent Magni to deliver his last message instead of summoning me. He doesn't want to be seen anywhere near me."

Aria had no rebuttal, and Radyn felt sorry she had to endure his ranting again. He'd made a choice after Nightkeep attacked, and he still thought it was the right one, but he hadn't realized the full extent of the price he'd have to pay. Now, they both had to suffer for it.

They both knew the conversation would lead nowhere, so Aria changed the subject, much to Radyn's relief. "Have you decided on whether or not you're going to volunteer for the bridge crews?"

Radyn ran his right hand through his hair. The farmers had talked about little else today, which contributed to his foul mood. "I don't think I should. Magni was clear about Jyn's desires, and the bridge crews interact quite a bit with the other cities. I know there's a huge need considering the number of bridges that need to be erected, but I think it's best if I don't take part."

Aria's face fell at his answer, but she didn't argue against him. He sensed an unresolved tension in her, a slight tightness across her shoulders that he didn't think had anything to do with him not wanting to work on the bridge crews. He resisted the temptation to pester her about it. She would talk to him when she felt the time was right.

He'd noticed the same tension in her more often lately, and her thoughts often seemed to wander when they were together. She was wrestling with a problem, but she didn't want to involve him yet. He respected her wishes and didn't press, but deep in his heart, he feared she tired of the situation they found themselves in. Her future was bright, but he didn't know where his led. The longer he worked in the fields, the less convinced he was that he belonged there. But he didn't know anything else. The paths of the clan were forever closed to him, but the occupation of his youth now held little appeal. What remained?

Aria lifted her head from his shoulder and shifted so that she was apart from him and looking straight at him. Her brow was furrowed slightly, and she licked her lips, sure signs she was planning on raising something big.

His heart seemed to skip several beats and his arms went cold, seized by a sudden panic stronger even than the fear he'd felt before battle. He knew with a crushing certainty that she was going to suggest separating. He'd considered it for weeks, wondering if it might be best for her, but it wasn't until this moment, when she was about to take the leap, that he realized how much he wanted to stay with her.

"I've been thinking about something since the news of the Gathering became public—" she began. She paused suddenly, which caused a stone to form in Radyn's throat.

He composed himself. He would respect her wishes, always, but he prepared his defenses.

"And I'm wondering if maybe it wouldn't be a good idea to apply to move to another city," she finished quickly, the words rushing out of her like water from a pitcher turned upside down.

Radyn opened his mouth, then blinked as what she said struck him. He closed his mouth and cocked his head to the side. "You want to move, with me?"

She frowned. "It wouldn't make much sense for me to move alone."

It felt like someone had taken his thoughts and thrown them in a deep pile of snow and frozen them solid. He stared at her, dumbfounded, until his thoughts started racing again. "You don't mean Nightkeep, do you?"

She laughed, but there was an edge to it, an uncertainty. She hadn't expected him to react as he was. "I'm guessing they wouldn't approve our request, unless it's to make killing you that much easier. No, I was thinking more about Starfall. Kleona has friends there, and she said she'd put in a good word if we wanted one."

Kleona was Aria's master, a demanding craftswoman but a kind soul. Aria had been considering this for a while, and seriously, too, if she'd brought it up to her master as a new apprentice.

Radyn leaned back and let his head rest against the wall. The idea of moving had never even occurred to him, though it probably should have. He tried to imagine a new life in a new city. The stain on his name would be wiped clean, and though it was unlikely Starfall would accept him as clan, he assumed he would be given leave to live peacefully as a farmer. Maybe that would make the difference.

Not only that, but he and Aria could start fresh in a place that would be new to both of them. A place where they could get married and start a family, like they'd talked about more times than he could count.

Except…

He looked away from Aria. Elora had given her life to save this city. She had spent the last years of her life training him to protect it. All he'd sacrificed was his reputation. If he left, wouldn't that be a betrayal of her trust in him?

"It's a tempting idea," Radyn admitted, "but I'm not sure."

Aria's eyes flashed. She blew out a frustrated breath and pushed herself off the couch. Her book, the center of her attention a moment ago, fell to the floor, its binding open and its pages bent. He expected her to shout at him but then decided it was worse that she didn't. She put her hands on her hips and stared at him.

"You need to choose," she said. It was a gently worded command, but he knew he would obey. Few orders had ever come with so much weight.

"If you want to keep living in Firestone because you think you owe it to Elora and to your father, that's fine. You know what to expect. Nothing much is going to change, and I can't stand the way you keep moping around feeling sorry for yourself."

She held up a hand to forestall his arguments. "The deal you made with Jyn helped keep the city together. I'm proud of you for making that choice, but these are the consequences. Either accept them and move on or leave this city and move on."

"I—" he didn't know what to say.

She kneeled in front of him. "I'm not asking you to decide this minute, though it'll be easier if you decide faster. But you need to choose. I'm happy to follow you either way. The only future I won't be a part of is the one where you keep going on as you are, thinking that something is going to change for you. The only way the world changes is when we change it."

Radyn bowed his head, helpless against Aria's wisdom. He nodded. "I will. I promise."

A tight grin turned the corners of Aria's mouth up. "I knew you would. Sometimes, it just takes a little kick. And I think you should be a part of the bridge-building crew. You've never seen a Gathering before, have you?"

Radyn shook his head. The last one had been when he'd been too young to remember.

"It's an incredible sight. You'd be ashamed to miss it."

Radyn wasn't sure if defying Jyn's wishes was wise, especially if he wanted to continue living in peace within Firestone. But Aria was also right. He wanted to be on the surface, helping to prepare for the Gathering as the cities neared. "That's an order, isn't it?"

Aria grinned wider. "Yes, it is. Now get up. We've got a meal to eat and I'm getting hungry."

Radyn stood and offered a mock bow. "Yes, ma'am. Lead the way."

3

———

The sun rose higher in the sky than it had during harvest, so Radyn knew the Singers had directed Firestone south for the Gathering. This cycle's harvest was nearly completed, so only a handful of farmers remained in the barren fields. In a typical year, Radyn would have been able to walk from one edge of the surface to the other without seeing more than a handful of clan guards. He'd looked forward to the end of harvest and a few weeks of quiet.

Unfortunately, "quiet" was the last word anyone would use to describe the surface today. "Chaotic, loud, and crowded" more accurately described the mass of laborers preparing the grounds for the Gathering.

Behind him, the strongest farmers hauled on pulleys that lifted heavy materials from storage rooms near the bottom of the city, and various crafters supervised the construction of temporary structures and the enormous bridges that would connect the cities once they were close. As Radyn understood the plan, the three cities of

Nightkeep would each connect to various points on Firestone's south-facing side, while Starfall would connect to the opposite side. Radyn couldn't guess at the logic of the configuration, but as Magni had made clear before the Gathering had even been announced, it wasn't his concern.

Radyn and a group of farmers assembled the pieces that would form one of the main bridges. Sturdy pipes, heavy cable, and thin but strong platforms were painstakingly cleaned and then assembled. Radyn's hands were dark, with years of accumulated dust and sweat beaded down his forehead. Earlier in the day, he'd made the mistake of attempting to wipe the sweat from his brow, and now his face was dirty, too.

Dozens of dragons filled the sky. Messengers passed back and forth between the approaching cities so frequently that he wondered if the dragons were starting to tire. The clan had strict rules for how often the dragons were to be flown, including in times of war, but barely a minute passed when the shadow of one didn't pass overhead.

The preparations might have been chaotic, but Firestone's progress was visible and consistent. Building the bridge was back-breaking work, but many hands made the work bearable, and the excitement surrounding the Gathering made Radyn feel as though he had his hand on a shard again. The air crackled with anticipation.

The fact it was anticipation and not worry spoke volumes about Jyn's leadership. He'd announced the Gathering at a city-wide assembly, and he'd fielded no shortage of questions from concerned citizens. Radyn wasn't sure if the assembly had been convinced by Jyn's logic or by the sheer force of his presence. Gatherings were considered sacred by all, and if Nightkeep was bold enough to break the truce, even it might not stand against the repercussions the other cities would enforce. Even so, there were lots of ways to harm a city without attacking it outright, and Nightkeep had already proven its willingness to stoop low to achieve their aims.

At a shout from a neighboring worker, Radyn looked up from the half-completed bridge to watch the southern sky. Miles and miles away, thick clouds gathered, but at least one sharp eye had noticed the faint, dark outline of Nightkeep's three cities. Radyn watched as the leading city broke through, streaming tangled wisps of cloud behind it. The other two followed close behind, both slightly higher in altitude. Their outlines grew quickly.

Radyn's gut tightened at the sight. Under any other circumstance, Firestone would be ordering their dragons to the sky to protect the city. A year ago, he and Tanwen would have been racing to battle. His grip tightened on his hammer as though it were a hilt. No bells rang as the enemy cities grew closer.

He tried to return to work, but his attention kept getting pulled back to the southern skies. He'd never seen another city while he stood upon the surface of Firestone. The only time he'd seen another city at all was when he'd spotted Nightkeep in the sky just before they hit Firestone.

The sight of the three cities sent a shiver down his spine despite the warmth of the day. He trusted Jyn and his judgment, but he couldn't bring himself to accept that having Nightkeep anywhere close to Firestone was a wise idea. They'd spent invaluable lives and resources to bring Firestone down once before. Why make it easier for them to try again?

Orders came down from the foreman to finish the final preparations to extend the bridge. Radyn watched Nightkeep longer than the others, certain that the moment he looked away, Nightkeep's dragons would rise, prepared to attack. Eventually, though, his help was needed, and he bent to his task.

He understood this all had been done before, but the enormity of the task overwhelmed him. The cities were as large as small mountains, and though he didn't doubt the skill of Firestone's Singers, they'd have to direct the city to within a hundred feet of Nightkeep to ensure a successful bridge crossing. Nightkeep's and Starfall's Singers would have to do the same until all five cities floated in the air together. That level of control, even for the Singers, seemed impossible.

Yet they were going to try. Nightkeep's three cities quickly grew larger, and Radyn wasn't alone as he stared. Most here had never seen a whole city from top to bottom. Even those who worked on the surface only ever saw a fraction of Firestone, much less those who spent most of their lives in the tunnels that honeycombed the inside of their city.

Nightkeep had the same basic design as Firestone. It was shaped like a child's top and expanded until it could protect thousands of citizens from the dangers of the world's surface. Radyn assumed the passages below were similar but was unlikely to find out for sure. He was willing to push the limits of his freedom here in Firestone, but the clans would never let him onto Nightkeep. If they did, it would only be to make his assassination that much easier.

Once the bridge was ready, there was nothing more to do until the cities were in position. Radyn looked around to ensure no one paid him much attention, then closed his eyes and opened his connection to the shards hidden within his flesh. He listened for the Song of the Engine far below his feet. It didn't take long to find. His daily training with Elora had become little more than fond memories, but the discipline she'd instilled in him continued long past her death. He was more sensitive to the Song now than he had been when she'd been alive. He didn't dare dive too deep, all too aware the Singers would discover him if he did. Instead, he skimmed along the surface, forcing himself to be content with gentle impressions and soft notes.

Even without plunging headfirst into the deep waters of the Song, he thought it was the most beautiful music he'd ever heard.

The Singers were in the midst of their own song, directing the Engine to the place where they would meet with Nightkeep. As usual, their song was discordant to Radyn's senses. They were like children, trying to duplicate the subtle beauty of the Engine's music but failing completely. Even so, the Engine responded to their crude efforts, and Firestone glided to a slow and comfortable stop, barely even noticeable on the surface.

As the cities of Nightkeep drew closer, Radyn was

surprised to find that he could hear their Engines as well. Compared to the sweet melodies of Firestone's Engine, Nightkeep's Engines sounded like an out-of-tune instrument. Radyn winced, then closed himself off from the Songs. He knew himself well. If left to himself, he'd dive into the Songs until he was so deep there was nothing left of him.

Whatever difficulties Nightkeep experienced with their Engines, it wasn't apparent to Radyn's eyes. The cities grew until they filled most of the sky. When they were within a mile of Firestone, they started to slow and bleed off some of their altitude.

Radyn had plenty of time to observe. The incredible strength of the Engines was on full display as the cities gathered, but starting and stopping the enormous cities was no easy feat. It felt like half the morning had passed by the time Nightkeep was in position.

Radyn assumed the order to extend the bridges would come soon, but he took a moment to connect once more with his shards. Firestone's Singers had halted their song, their city in position. Nightkeep's Singers continued their attempts, which sounded more like angry parents shouting at misbehaving children than the gentle and subtle songs that represented the peak of a Singer's ability.

Regardless of the quality of their singing, Nightkeep's Singers wrestled their city into position successfully. Soon, their voices went thankfully silent. Radyn closed himself off from his shards, certain the order to extend the bridges was forthcoming.

It was. The order to prepare came only a few minutes

after he disconnected from his shards. He and all the other builders took positions alongside the bridge, ready to guide it toward its new resting place. They weren't far from the clan's dragon nests, so Radyn saw Firestone's dragons take flight, two clan Swords on their backs. The pair of dragons circled high above once, then came down to land near the edge of the city so that specially-made harnesses could be fit to them.

The harnesses were connected to heavy wires that stretched to the leading tip of the bridge. At the signal from their riders, both dragons took to the air again, rising until they'd taken all the slack out of the wire.

The bridge had been constructed on top of a long line of cylinders that allowed it to be pulled and pushed back and forth. Orders came down the line to push, and Radyn and the other builders put their backs into the effort. He'd originally thought the dragons would do most of the pulling, but he was quickly disabused of that notion. The dragons didn't pull so much as rise, keeping the tip of the bridge high enough to reach Nightkeep as the laborers pushed.

Every few feet, Radyn and the others paused as a team of burly men attached hooks and rope to the forward-most cylinder the bridge rolled upon. Then Radyn and the others would resume pushing. Fortunately, Radyn was on the south side of the bridge, so he could watch the cylinder teams working. The teams let the cylinder ride right off the edge of Firestone, then halted its descent with their ropes and pulled it back to the surface.

The now-unused cylinders were left to the side and

became a mark of their continued progress. Soon, Radyn found himself close to the edge. The engineer in charge ordered him away from his position and to the back of the bridge, where he continued pushing.

His legs burned and sweat dripped down his brow as he helped push the massive bridge. The temptation to tap into his shards was always there, the strength and stamina of a Sword always just a thought away, but he kept his discipline.

The order came to stop, and anchors were driven deep into the ground, reaching all the way to the stone that served as the ceiling to the first level below. A set of stairs was moved into place, and one of the builders rushed up them, leaped to the bridge, and threw his hands high into the air. The antics were met with a smattering of cheers and laughter, but it wasn't long before a pair of Daggers came to interrupt the fun. They gently escorted the man back down into the crowd.

Radyn shook his head and looked beyond his immediate surroundings. This bridge was hardly the only one in progress. One would be built to each of Nightkeep's cities, as well as to Starfall. Daggers and Swords spread out to guard the bridges, which now directly connected Firestone to the city that had once tried to kill them all. At least that time, Nightkeep had been forced to sacrifice clan and dragon lives to reach Firestone.

Eventually, Shields would take over, ensuring everyone had the proper documents to cross, but for now, the task fell exclusively to the clan. The engineer in charge of the bridge shouted more orders. A group of workers carrying long poles and netting reported to him. He gestured in turn at specific workers, then pointed at different parts of the bridge. The workers bowed and stepped onto the bridge, inserting the poles in holes in the bridge designed for the purpose. They then began stretching the net from pole to pole, making the bridge that much safer for citizens to travel back and forth. Radyn supposed it wouldn't be much of a Gathering if people were constantly being blown off the bridges to their deaths.

He watched for a few minutes longer, but he wasn't part of the safety crew, so his role was finished. He was forgotten as the others gathered around him to plan their celebrations. He yawned and rubbed his eyes. Building the bridge and getting it into position had consumed his efforts the past few days, and he decided he'd earned something of a rest. Maybe he'd go home, clean up, and surprise Aria in her workroom.

As he turned toward the nearest stair, a brief glimpse of a familiar but unexpected face froze him in his tracks.

Jelrik and a handful of companions strode purposefully toward the nest. Radyn moved so a small group of celebrating builders was between him and Jelrik. He was glad he'd been in the middle of a crowd, as dirty and sweaty as everyone nearby. Jelrik almost certainly hadn't seen him. Radyn had been fortunate to spot Jelrik before he was lost to the crowd.

He watched the Singer as guilt reached its cold hand into his chest and twisted. A year ago, he would have counted Jelrik as a friend and a trusted ally. But he hadn't seen the Singer once since Elora had died. Jyn had told him that Jelrik blamed him for Elora's death, and Radyn had no trouble believing that was true. He'd written letters and requested audiences, but Jelrik's answering silence spoke volumes.

All the feelings he'd suffered through in those first days after the battle returned as though he'd never dealt with them at all. They'd won the battle, and Elora had saved the city, but it still felt like they'd lost, and it was all Radyn's fault.

It never helped that most of the city already believed essentially that. It was all too easy to accept he was exactly what so many people believed of him.

A small part of him wanted to cry out for Jelrik, to beg for forgiveness. But Jelrik's behavior made Radyn pause. He first noticed that Jelrik wasn't wearing the robes of a Singer. By itself, that meant little. There weren't any rules that said a Singer always had to wear their robes in public.

But now that Radyn had identified Jelrik, he noticed some of the others following him. Two of them were Singers that he recognized, and if three were Singers, it stood to reason most or all of them were.

They passed through the gate to the nest with nothing more than a brief bow from the guards at the gate, further solidifying Radyn's suspicions. Those grounds were some of the most closely protected in Firestone, and for good reason. If Jelrik had been wearing his robes, Radyn might not have questioned the quick passage, but now he looked to be nothing more than a well-off civilian. That the guards let him through so quickly implied they'd been expecting his arrival.

Radyn drifted from group of workers to group of workers, never pausing long enough to attract much attention. Thankfully, he didn't have to wait long, which meant again that this visit had been expected. Dragons could take a while to prepare.

An entire flight of dragons left the nest, dropping quickly out of sight after they took off. Radyn let his eyes wander. It was possible the Singers were traveling to the surface, which would also be interesting, but he wanted to be sure.

He saw them again a few minutes later, rising on the backside of one of Nightkeep's cities and coming in for a landing. Radyn lost sight of them, then, and figured he wouldn't find them again anytime soon.

He turned again for the nearest stairwell, still intending to wash up and surprise Aria. But now his steps were slower as he worked through what he'd just seen.

There was one question he wanted the answer to more than any other:

Why had Jelrik and some of Firestone's best Singers snuck out of Firestone and onto Nightkeep on dragons when there was a perfectly good bridge for them to cross?

4

———

The smell of the food from the kitchens made Kaya's mouth water and her stomach rumble. The last time she'd eaten a full meal, she'd been living with Father and Mother, but even those meals had been uncommon. Particularly near the end, Father had been nervous to let her into public places, so he'd had meals brought to her. By the time it reached her mouth, it had long since gone cold. Hunger was often preferable to the slop that covered her plate.

At least it meant she had practice for the trials she now faced. This city's kitchens made incredible stews, recipes that filled the halls with pleasant scents of roasting meat and fresh herbs. She'd have given almost anything to fill her stomach with one of those meals, but the shadow was here, too, strong enough to haunt her even during daylight hours.

She wrapped her arms around her legs and squeezed them tight, hoping the rumbling of her stomach wouldn't attract attention from anyone passing by in the adjacent hallway. The access tunnel that served as her most recent hiding place had regularly placed vents that expelled warm air into the hallways. They made good sleeping places, but any sound she made traveled up and down the hall.

When it felt like her stomach wasn't going to betray her again, she turned her thoughts to the problem at hand. She needed food. Water had been easy enough to find, and shelter was as simple as choosing her hiding place for the day. She never dared stay in one place for long, but there were always plenty of places to choose from.

It always came down to food. It had been two days since she'd risked discovery to sneak into a kitchen at night and devour what scraps she could find. She'd almost been spotted by a cook, and she hadn't dared try again. But now, the cramps in her stomach demanded attention.

She'd thought food would be the least of her worries. She'd thought, at first, that she would simply find a kitchen, sneak into line, and eat a meal without anyone being the wiser. It wasn't as though anyone tracked the meals or the guests.

Her age worked against her. If she were a few years older, the sight of a young woman eating by herself wouldn't raise an eyebrow. But she was too young and looked even younger than she was, and they were looking for her. The moment she stepped into one of the city's dining rooms alone, she'd be spotted. Even if she wasn't arrested, people would notice her, and it would lead her pursuers to her location.

Her stomach rumbled again, making her doubt the wisdom of her choices. Why had she listened to the Song? At least with Father, she'd gotten meals, even if they were cold.

She shook her head. Her thoughts often traveled in those directions, but they did her no good. She'd been right to flee. Comfort was one of the shadow's greatest allies. It turned good people soft, robbing them of the strength to face shadow's challenges.

The hallway she hid near led to one of the larger kitchens in the city, and she had her face pressed close to one of the vents. There was no lack of food in the city. She just needed to find a way to take some.

The kitchens were regularly resupplied with food, and there weren't any guards on the food as it moved from the storage rooms below to the kitchens. Unfortunately, there was no way she could think of to steal the food in transit without being noticed. She'd explored the idea of robbing from the storage rooms below, but she didn't know where in the vast underbelly of the city the food was stored. In time, she might learn, but she was starving now.

She'd also imagined no small number of daring raids on the kitchen, but they were guarded by Shields. It wasn't impossible to sneak into one, but close to it. She'd been lucky not to get caught the one time she tried.

If she couldn't get to the food on its way into the kitchen or while it was in the kitchen, her only remaining opportunity was to snatch it afterward, which was what she hoped to accomplish tonight. Surely the staff had to dispose of the leftover food somewhere.

Once she figured out where, she could eat like a queen of old.

The only problem was that she'd been watching the kitchens all day and hadn't seen any food come out. She bit her lower lip. Perhaps there was a chute they threw it down?

Night fell as the lights dimmed. Should she try a different approach?

Her stomach rumbled yet again, and she clenched at it. She couldn't delay much longer.

Moving slowly, she wormed her way down the access tunnel, careful not to make much noise. Eventually, she came to a ladder, which she descended into a small room. She put her ear to the door, then closed her eyes and listened to the guidance of the Song. Perhaps she was a fool, trusting it even after it had led her here, but there was little else for her to trust.

The Song gave her nothing. The Engine in this city was different than her own, but its melodies were just as broken. The Song that ran beneath that of the Engine remained unbroken, but it didn't offer her the guidance she craved. Fortunately, she didn't hear anything through the door either, so she stepped out into the hallway.

Her clothes were dirty, her hair was unkempt, and she smelled, but she didn't know how to solve any of those problems while remaining unseen. She hurried down the hall with her eyes cast down, grateful that most people in the area were tucked away tightly in their homes.

If she was going to find food, it was more likely going to be around one of the small kitchens. The large ones would have the most guards and the most activity.

Thankfully, the hallways of this city weren't laid out any differently than those of Nightkeep. She'd never been here before a few days ago, but she knew the layout as though she were walking the cold halls of her home city.

She walked small hallways and side passages as often as she could. The larger hallways that served as thoroughfares would have been faster, but they'd be filled with people even at this late hour.

Kaya couldn't avoid people completely. She passed two young men in the hallway, but neither were clan or Shields, so she bowed quietly as they passed and hurried on. It was possible they might remember her if questioned later, but it wouldn't help her pursuit much. They already knew she was in their city.

She still remembered the moment she'd opened her eyes and found herself in a different Engine room. She'd known because she was alone and because the Song of the Engine was unlike any she'd heard before. After taking a moment to ensure she was actually alive, she stepped out of the Engine room to the great surprise of the two Swords standing guard on the other side of the door.

There'd been a commotion and plenty of finger-pointing, each of the Swords convinced the other had somehow failed in their duty. She supposed she'd been lucky there was so little trust between them. She'd claimed it was all a prank, an effort organized by the children to see if anyone could sneak into an Engine room.

Eventually, one of the Swords insisted he was going to drag her back to her parents and demand an explanation.

She'd agreed, but once they were alone, she'd run. The Sword had pursued for a time, but the Song strengthened Kaya's legs, and her desire to escape was stronger than his desire to catch her.

So, there was no doubt they knew. That, plus the presence of the shadow, meant she would be hunted. She'd escaped it once but doubted she could do so again. Allies could come after food, though.

She descended a small ladder that deposited her not far from one of the smaller kitchens on the seventh level. Instead of bothering with the main entrance, Kaya worked her way to the back, toward the entrance that the cooks used.

Her heart pounded faster in her chest when she saw the door was unguarded. She hurried to it and pressed her ear against the wood. At the same time, she closed her eyes to listen for the Song. She doubted it would guide her in this matter, and she was right. It was beautiful, harmonious, and right but offered no directions.

Kaya took a deep breath, tensed her muscles, and opened the door. It squeaked as it opened, the sound deafening in the silence of the past few minutes. She winced, but there was nothing to do except push it open wide enough so that she could slip through. Once through, she listened for the sound of anyone approaching, but the kitchen was silent.

She elected to leave the door open, judging the squeakiness of the door as a greater threat to her discovery than the door left open behind her. She stepped into the kitchen, ready to eat anything she could get her hands on.

Her eyes went wide at the treasure trove she'd stumbled upon. It looked like someone had been making a sandwich and given up halfway through. Tomatoes were neatly sliced on a cutting board next to three thin slices of what looked like steak. A third of a loaf of bread lay next to the cutting board as though welcoming her home.

Her eyes darted around the room. She hadn't heard anyone since she entered, and that remained true. She strained her ears, almost certain this was a trap.

Except that was silly. There were more than a dozen kitchens in the city, and no one even knew what neighborhoods she'd been haunting. More than likely, someone had been working here and had to leave for some reason. No self-respecting cook would leave their work area like this, so she had to hurry.

They'd be back soon.

She grabbed the meat first and stuffed it in her mouth. At a glance, it hadn't seemed like anything special. As a Singer's daughter, she'd been given some of the very best of what Nightkeep had to offer. But she was certain she'd never tasted a cut of beef half as delicious as this one. She chewed fast, hoping to empty her mouth quickly so she could stuff it full again.

As she chewed, she looked around for something to stash the rest of the food in. She ripped the bread into pieces small enough to fit in her pockets, and as soon as she'd swallowed the beef, she ate the tomatoes.

A small voice in the back of her head warned her that

she was eating too much too fast and that if she were wise, she'd save some for later, but she was thinking with her stomach only. Tomorrow's problems could stay there, for all she cared.

It only took her a few minutes to clear the counter of all the food.

She turned around to search for anything else that had been left out, then froze. An old woman stood behind her, long gray hair tied in a knot behind her head. Her eyes crinkled as she smiled at Kaya. "Nothing to worry about, girl. Name's Robyn, and I don't think I've seen anyone so eager to eat some of my cooking since the days of famine."

Her voice was kind, but Kaya couldn't stay. Robyn was positioned in such a way that Kaya could run right past her and reach the door in no time at all. She didn't know how she hadn't heard the cook, but she wouldn't stay long enough to regret her mistake.

Robyn held up a hand and said the only words that could have stopped her. "If you stay, I'd be happy to fix you something more. It won't be anything fancy, mind you, but it should fill that hole in your belly where a stomach is supposed to be."

Kaya felt torn in two directions at once. This cook had seen her. She would know Kaya was hungry and would tell the Shields to watch the other kitchens. Kaya had to run now and raid them before the Shields could double their guards and lock the kitchens down even tighter than they were already.

But she promised food now, and though the Song

didn't tell her anything useful, she struck Kaya as having a kind heart.

She debated, inching toward the door but wanting to stay. Robyn had the wisdom not to say anything more, knowing somehow that if she did, Kaya would use it as an excuse to bolt. She stood still, not making any attempt to block Kaya's exit.

It was that, more than anything, that convinced her. She gave Kaya a choice, even when she deserved none.

The tension dropped from her body. Robyn had already seen her, so the damage was done. She might as well get a meal out of the deal. She bowed to her. "I'd be very grateful, thank you."

A wide grin broke out on her face. "All that hunger and still so well-mannered? Girl, I'm going to make you a feast the like you'll be telling your grandchildren about someday."

5

———

Radyn stopped beside Aria as she strode confidently to the side of the bridge. A steady flow of people walked from one city to the other, but Aria paid them no mind as she grabbed the railing and pressed her face into the netting. Radyn took half a step forward to stop her, then stopped and tried to act as though he wasn't nervous.

There was little to worry about. The Gathering was already in its second day and the bridges hadn't so much as shivered since they'd been anchored. He didn't always have kind words to share about the Singers, but they'd done remarkable work bringing the cities together. The mighty Engines held the cities perfectly still in relation to one another.

At least for now. Radyn didn't worry about Firestone's Engine. It ran stronger now than it had in years, thanks to Elora's sacrifice. The other cities' Engines didn't inspire much confidence, though. Radyn listened to bits and pieces of their Songs when he could, and none were healthy. So as Aria stared eagerly through the netting, Radyn reached out with his senses to Tanwen. The dragon rested comfortably in the nest, but he reassured Radyn he'd come running if the bridge were to fail.

The joy on Aria's face washed away some of his concerns. "Incredible," she said softly.

Radyn stepped closer to the railing so he could share the moment with her. The land was far below, thick with wild forest. They were too high to make out many details, but if one stretched their gaze to the horizon, they could see the slight curve of their world.

Radyn reminded himself that although the sight wasn't new to him, Aria had never seen anything like it. She'd ridden on a dragon once when he, Astram, and Bergen had rescued her and her roommates from the ruins of Whitehawk. But that flight had been at night, so she'd never had the opportunity to see the world this way. She wasn't one that liked visiting the lower observation deck. He'd asked her why once, and she'd answered that she didn't like being reminded that she wasn't on solid ground.

Radyn couldn't imagine what it was like for her, having survived the fall of Whitehawk, and a selfish part of him hoped he never would.

She couldn't disguise her delight at the vista that stretched before her, though. Radyn thought she looked a bit like a child, but he appreciated her sense of wonder. Becoming a rider had spoiled him.

She wasn't the only person with their face pressed to the net. Up and down the bridge, families crowded along the railing to witness the sight. Most of their faces were filled with a variety of stunned disbelief. Day to day, it was easy to forget the reality of their existence. Everyone knew they were in a floating city, alive only thanks to the ancient makers and their magnificent Engines. But Aria wasn't alone in her preferences. Few ever peered off the edge of the city or visited the observation deck at the bottom of Firestone. Even the farmers who diligently toiled upon the surface rarely wandered so close to the edge they would know they were flying. The motion of the city was so gentle that, except for rare occasions, it felt as if the city was still.

The bridge reminded everyone of the truth, and Radyn considered that good. The closer people lived to the truth, the better off they were.

While Aria stared, he turned his attention to the crowd flowing between the cities. He decided there was one easy way of classifying the travelers, and that was by how they crossed the bridge. Perhaps a third were like Aria, drawn to the railing of the bridge to bask in a rare sight. But the other two-thirds stuck close to the middle of the bridge, refusing to look either left or right. Many feared heights, but some, Radyn imagined, simply hated being reminded that they lived in the sky.

Regardless of their feelings, the mood on the bridge was festive. Gatherings were rare occasions, and this one was still in its earliest stages. No concluding date had been announced yet, but if history were any guide, it would be a week or two distant.

Those weeks would be wildly busy. Merchants, crafters, and farmers would flock from one city to another to see what they could trade. Nightkeep was sure to be rich in resources and supplies that were harder to find on Firestone. No small multitude of sins could be easily forgiven in exchange for fresh herbs, refined ores, and liquors that were impossible to find in Firestone's establishments.

He grunted at the thought. If Jyn really did want to strike a lasting peace with Nightkeep, a Gathering was a clever way of going about it. Especially once the planned feasts and celebrations began. Marriages tended to spike within the months following a Gathering, and a flood of babies usually arrived not long after that.

Thinking of all the new mothers made him turn his attention back to Aria. She was still lost in the grandeur of the vista, and her wonder brought a smile to his face. She didn't deserve the hardship and privation she'd endured because of him. Perhaps he was a fool to cling so tightly to Firestone. Maybe she was right, and they should consider applying for citizenship upon Starfall.

She finally broke her gaze away from the landscape and turned to him. "You're lucky to see views like this so often."

"I was lucky," he corrected her.

It was the wrong thing to say, and he knew it the moment the words passed his lips. Her smile fell and the light in her eyes dimmed. He hurried to recover. "I'm sorry, that slipped out. I *am* lucky, even though I miss Tanwen."

Some of her joy returned, but it wasn't as unrestrained as before, and Radyn cursed himself. He focused too much on what he had lost and not nearly enough on what he still possessed. Aria was still with him, but if he wasn't careful, who knew how much longer that would last?

He took her hand. "Come. Let's see if the Starfall crafters are talented enough to impress you."

She let herself be pulled along, and slowly, the smile returned to her face. Thankfully, they had no problems with the Shields at the other end of the bridge. Their papers earned nothing more than a brief glance and then they were across and in a new city.

It was more different than Radyn expected. After his experiences within the halls of Whitehawk and the mysterious settlement Melanie had shown him on the surface, he had come to expect that all cities were mostly the same. Starfall quickly distinguished itself, though, and Radyn found himself possessed by the same sense of wonder Aria had felt just moments before.

Running not far from where the bridge was anchored was a small stream. Radyn wandered over to it, staring at the deep groove that channeled the water. It flowed into a pond located close to the edge of the city.

Radyn watched the water, studied the pond, and scratched at his chin. "That doesn't make any sense," he said.

"Why not?" Aria asked.

Radyn pointed at the stream. "The water goes down into the pond, but the height of the pond never changes. Shouldn't it overflow and soak their fields?"

Aria laughed. "There's a hole in the bottom of the pond that keeps a steady water level. The water is then pushed through pipes and brought back to the surface so it can flow down the stream again. It's one of the distinguishing features of Starfall."

Radyn shook his head. "Incredible." There was no running water on the surface of Firestone. Farmers could request emergency water from Firestone's massive holds for irrigation, but the practice was frowned upon. The Singers did their best to send the city through storms to replenish water supplies and keep the soil healthy.

Aria let him watch for a moment longer, then pulled on his arm. "Come on. I've heard that Starfall has access to some of the best mining land in the world. I want to look at their gems."

Radyn let himself be pulled. Like on Firestone, tables had been carried up from below and an impromptu market thrived as the cities' populations mixed together. Radyn hadn't brought anything to trade. He only owned one item of value, which was hidden safely in their room back in Firestone. Other farmers from Firestone had helped themselves to select quantities of more uncommon herbs and spices, but Radyn hadn't bothered. He hadn't been sure he'd even be given access, but more to the point, he didn't feel any need to trade. He already had everything he wanted. Aria, though, had crafted a handful of items she thought would make excellent trades. She was eager to access minerals and supplies that were hard to get in Firestone.

Had it been his decision alone, he wouldn't have come to the market. Sure, they had goods he'd never seen before, but they were all only things and as such, held little of his attention. But Aria had persuaded him it would be a good use of their time, and to no one's surprise, she'd been right. He grinned as he watched her haggle with a gemsmith. When she gestured, he slipped the pack off his back and handed it to her.

She pulled out a small lamp. At a glance, it didn't appear much different than any other, but once Aria launched into her offer, the gemsmith wouldn't have a chance.

"It's a lamp that charges itself from the energy of any nearby lamps. All you have to do is set it close and leave it for at least an hour. After that, it will hold the charge for weeks. If there's ever an emergency and the lamps go out in your home, you'll be able to use this without problem."

Radyn smiled and shook his head. He'd witnessed enough variations of the exchange to know how it would end. Aria could sell firewood to a lumberjack, though she never claimed to be great at selling. Instead of watching fate take its course, Radyn turned his attention to the market.

The place was bustling, filled with people from all walks of life. A few intrepid individuals had set up food stands, trading snacks and treats with hungry passersby. Many people were haggling, much as Aria was, but there were a fair number of people simply walking around and enjoying the sights. Strangers introduced themselves as they passed.

Radyn couldn't think of another time he'd seen so many people on the surface of any city. It was more people than he liked being around, but the joviality of the Gathering infected him despite his efforts to remain aloof. He was even glad that he wasn't allowed around

Nightkeep. As the far larger city, it would be even more packed with people.

His eyes narrowed as something tugged on the edges of his awareness. He turned, and as he did, he caught a flash of dark hair in the sun. A young girl sprinted away from him, as though he'd caught her in the middle of a crime. He followed her with his gaze as she hid behind a stall and stopped. Had she been watching him? She was small, though, not much older than a child.

She hid behind a pair of adults haggling with a merchant, then turned on her heel and walked away, carefully keeping the adults between her and Radyn. He took a step to the side so that he could watch her. She was a slim girl who looked like she didn't eat enough. Her clothes appeared to be of fine quality, but they were dirtier than Radyn's old clothes after a day full of bloody training.

She turned into a stairwell and disappeared. Radyn considered following her, then shook his head. The quality of the clothes and their condition made him curious, but following a girl because she'd been staring at him hardly made sense.

He turned back to Aria in time to watch her successfully trade two of her lamps for a pile of gems. He couldn't imagine what she would do with the new acquisitions, but he didn't ask. She liked to surprise him with her creations.

It would be a shame to leave Firestone, he decided. She'd just made a home there and had found a master who treated her well. She'd certainly do well if they moved to Starfall, of course, but it would mean starting over again, and he couldn't ask that of her. He'd already asked far too much. She was right, though. He'd have to find his own way forward.

They browsed a few more stalls together before Aria suggested they head down into the heart of the city. There was a craftsman she wanted to visit, and she'd heard rumors of another market down below.

Radyn wasn't eager to be trapped within the confines of a foreign city, but he couldn't say no to Aria. The smile on her face looked like it had been glued there, and he hadn't seen her this happy for weeks. He nodded and she pulled him after her.

That smile sealed his decision. They'd stay on Firestone and find a way to live in peace. This relationship was too precious to waste.

They were halfway to the nearest stairwell when Radyn sensed a commotion behind them. It wasn't marked by shouts or screams, but by a rippling silence that spread through the market. Radyn turned to see a group of six Starfall Shields, accompanied by two Swords, marching toward him.

Aria's grip tightened on his hand. Familiar reflexes, unused for months, returned to his body. He shook his hand free of Aria's and took a long, sweeping look at his surroundings. The stairwell was close, but then he was locking himself in a cage with them. The bridge was also no good. It would certainly be closed to him.

They could leap off the edge and trust Tanwen to catch them, but not only was that unbelievably risky, he couldn't imagine what came after. He supposed some smaller city far away might accept a disgraced Sword on a dragon, but he doubted it. He and Aria would be hunted anywhere they went. They'd have to find a home on the surface, and he wouldn't subject her to that.

He released a slow breath and let the tension drain from his body.

"Are you the Firestone resident known as Radyn?" the commander of the Shields asked him.

"I am. Can I help you?"

The officer held out a pair of manacles. "Turn around and put your hands behind your back. You're under arrest for murder."

6

———————

Robyn was as good as her word and better. Not only did she feed Kaya that evening, but she invited Kaya to her apartment so she could shower and get a proper night's rest. Under other circumstances, she might have been more worried, but Robyn's food and good cheer eliminated any of her remaining objections. She was tired, dirty, and hungry, and Robyn promised to solve all three problems at once.

She followed Robyn to her home, which wasn't far from where the kitchen was located. It was a small place, but everywhere Kaya looked, she saw the home of a kindly widow. Sketches of a much younger Robyn and another young man hung from the walls, and a small desk filled with drawing supplies was tucked into the corner of the room.

Robyn smiled when she saw Kaya looking at the desk, and that smile told Kaya all she needed to know about her generous host. "That was Arthur's favorite place in the world. I can't tell you the number of times I came home to find him hunched over that desk, working on some new idea. He probably forgot to eat more times than he remembered, and he always said it was good he married a cook because otherwise he would have wasted away."

"When did he die?" Kaya asked.

"A few years back. Took a cold one day and all the healers in the city couldn't do a thing for him. But he lived well in the time he had. Died with grin on his face, and that's all anyone can ask, right?"

Kaya nodded, thinking of the mother she would never know.

"Come on. Let's get you showered. Would you like me to wash those clothes?"

Kaya clutched the worn fabric tight. The woman was only trying to help, but her clothes were the last thing she owned. The only possession she carried.

"It's fine, girl. Did you want to wash them yourself?"

Kaya nodded, and Robyn went to gather the supplies. She came back with soap and a washing board. "There's a spare towel in the bathroom. You can wash your clothes, then hop in the shower."

Kaya bowed. "Thank you."

Robyn waved her thanks away, but just before Kaya stepped into the bathroom, she saw the older woman walk over to the abandoned desk and run her hand along its surface.

Did Father grieve her disappearance? He was back on Nightkeep, so wouldn't know what had happened to her after she'd touched the Engine. As far as he knew, she'd died, just like any other Singer who dared to touch the Engine alone.

Somehow, she didn't think so. If he'd bothered at all, it would only be to pack up her room in a box to send to the market to be redistributed among other girls. He probably hadn't even shed a tear.

She closed the bathroom door harder than she meant to, then stripped off her clothes, washed them in the sink, and hung them up to dry. They were still too dirty but better than they'd been before. Next, she stepped in the shower and washed off the grime that had accumulated over the past several days. She basked in the feel of hot water running down her skin. The soft floral scents of the bar of soap almost brought tears to her eye.

When she came out, she realized she had a problem. Her clothes wouldn't be dry until at least tomorrow. Before she could decide, there was a knock on the door.

"I've got some spare clothes for you for tonight. They're probably a bit too large, but hopefully, they'll serve you well enough for sleeping."

Kaya pressed her forehead against the door, holding back the tears again. Robyn's simple kindness broke down the walls she'd built around her heart. She choked back a weak sob and said, "Thank you again."

She cracked open the door and Robyn passed the clothes through. Kaya put them on. As Robyn had predicted, they were too large, but they were soft and warm, like an embrace from a friend. Kaya stepped out of the bathroom only to be welcomed by Robyn's gentle smile.

"You look a lot better," she said.

"I feel a lot better," Kaya admitted.

Robyn gestured her toward the couch, which had been covered with blankets and a pillow. "It isn't much, and if I was younger, I'd offer you the bed, but these old bones don't recover the way they used to. I'm afraid it's the best I can offer."

"It's all very kind. Thank you."

Robyn nodded once as though she was satisfied with everything she saw. "I'm not the type to ask questions. If you want to tell me what you've been through, I'll always be a willing ear, but if you don't, that's fine, too. Do you have any plans?"

The question caught Kaya flat-footed. The last few days had been about nothing more than survival. She hadn't dared think far enough ahead to plan. She shook her head.

"Well, my door's always open. I'll be up early in the morning. I've got to prepare for the Gathering."

"Gathering?"

Robyn chuckled. "You really have been living under a rock. We're acting as a mediator between two cities that had a fight earlier in the year. Nightkeep is one, but what's the other?"

Kaya froze in place, ice running through her veins. She'd escaped, but now Nightkeep was coming here? Father and the others would hear that someone had escaped from the Engine room. She'd have the full weight of Nightkeep adding to her already impossible difficulties.

Robyn's attention was elsewhere. "Firestone! That was it. I'm not as familiar with that city, but we're already anchored with them. It's been the biggest Gathering anyone here can remember."

Her monologue ended when she saw Kaya's face. "Oh, dear, you look pale. Are you alright?"

Kaya gulped and nodded. "I think I'm just tired."

"Of course you are, dear. And here I am, prattling away. I guess it's been a long time since I've had company. You just rest. What I meant to say is that I'll be working most of the day tomorrow to prepare for the feasts, but if you'd like, I can sneak aside a few times to bring you meals. I do it enough for some on the council so no one will notice."

Kaya bowed deeply. "Thank you so much. You have no idea how much all of this means to me."

Robyn's answering smile warmed her heart. "Well, you get some sleep, and tomorrow will feel like a new beginning."

The first day with Robyn was the most relaxing and enjoyable day Kaya could remember having since she was much younger. She was nervous when Robyn left her alone, certain that her host would return with the Shields to arrest her. She paced the small living room all day, waiting for the end to come.

When the door opened and Robyn appeared with a plate of food, Kaya almost jumped out of her borrowed clothes.

"Sorry to give you such a fright, girl, but I brought you breakfast."

Kaya dug into the meal eagerly, and for the first time, her shoulders dropped, and she let herself breathe freely. She couldn't stay with Robyn forever. At some point, she'd need to leave and find her own way in the world. But with one last meal, Robyn had ensured that Kaya would always trust her. She'd had plenty of opportunities to betray this dirty, stray girl but hadn't.

Robyn returned to her work, but Kaya didn't mind. She turned her attention to the problems facing her, and her pacing became more contemplative than panicked.

One truth became immediately clear: she didn't want to simply survive. She wanted to build a life on the other side of the crisis that confronted her.

The shift in thinking wasn't an easy one to make. She had forgotten how long she had lived under her father's heavy thumb, and she'd become used to thinking in terms of the next minutes or hours. Planning for days or years felt as foreign as Robyn's kindness. She dreamed about what her home might look like and wondered if she would ever have a writing desk tucked away in the corner. She wondered if she would have a partner in her life in the same way that Robyn had Arthur's companionship. Before long, she found herself lost in visions of the future. But every time Robyn returned with more food, the harsh nature of her current reality reasserted itself. Planning for the future was all well and good, but it meant nothing if she couldn't survive the threats she faced today.

As day turned inexorably into night, one truth became clear: whatever the future held, she wouldn't discover it by hiding in Robyn's home. The woman had already done too much, and although Kaya didn't say anything to her host, she feared what consequences the cook might face.

She resolved that tomorrow, she would leave the apartment and visit the Gathering. She hadn't gotten all the stains out of her clothes, but they were cleaner than before, thanks to Robyn's showers, so she too would be presentable in any public gathering, and she wouldn't draw the same attention she would have earlier. Not only that, but the Gathering would serve as a wonderful cover. There would be so many people and strangers milling about in all corners of the city that it was less likely the Shields and the clan would notice her.

For the first time in years, Kaya fell asleep, eager to see what the next day would bring.

She woke early the next morning and left the apartment with Robyn. Her kind host had bags under her eyes and walked slower than usual, but the smile on her face was undiminished. As she'd warned, she'd worked late the night before, but today was supposed to be a short day, and then this afternoon, she planned on climbing to the surface and visiting one of the other cities.

Kaya parted ways with Robyn as they neared the kitchen, promising the older woman that she would return before the day's end. Her heart raced a little faster when Robyn disappeared around a corner, but she forced a smile onto her face and kept her chin up, acting as though she was any other young woman excited to experience the festivities of a Gathering.

Gatherings were a regular occurrence for Nightkeep. As the largest of the remaining cities, it had the most to trade, and smaller cities were always eager to meet with their big brother and exchange goods.

Kaya knew all of this to be true, but only because it had been taught to her by the numerous tutors who had instructed her over the years. She hadn't experienced any that she could remember clearly. Thankfully, that meant she didn't have to pretend to be excited for the festivities. She passed a few others who were also on the way and was reassured when none of them paid her the slightest mind. She reached the stairwell at the same time as a family and slipped right behind them so that she appeared to be one of their children. Her hair and pale complexion didn't match the family's, but she hoped the Shields wouldn't be paying close enough attention.

As she expected, at the top of the stairwell, a Shield stood guard, but instead of a stern glare and a sharp eye, he was talking with a young lady and laughing merrily. He didn't so much as glance her way as she passed.

She had to remind herself to keep moving when she saw the Gathering market for the first time. It was both smaller and quainter than she had expected, but it was all the more perfect for it. Sellers and buyers argued over prices, but both parties had smiles on their faces even as the arguments rose in volume.

Kaya wandered around the tables and the people. The various sellers captured her attention. Crafters sold everything from trinkets to jewelry. A handful of intrepid cooks sold snacks and unique breads that would never make their way into a city dining hall. The variety of people and work on display made her feel like a small child again, like the world was filled with possibility.

In Father's world, only the Singers mattered. The rest all existed so that the Singers could control the Engines. Once Kaya's gifts had been discovered, her world had become just as small. Out here, though, it was as wide and endless as the blue sky overhead. She could become a Singer, of course, but that decision was no longer written in stone. It would be her decision to make.

A gentle melody played softly as a couple passed her, and Kaya cocked her head to the side as she opened herself up to the Song. Her eyes widened.

The Song swirled around the man the same way it swirled around her, though he seemed oblivious to the harmonies that surrounded him. Not only that, but he had shards of an Engine buried inside his body. They burned like dim suns in her vision.

Despite her isolation, she'd interacted with plenty of people over the years, and she'd never encountered anyone like him. She separated from the Song and followed him from a distance.

To her sight, he and his companion didn't seem different than anyone else perusing the market that day. They stopped by several tables, and it appeared the man was being led by his partner. His eyes barely glanced at the various goods, but he turned his head often and looked around. Kaya stayed well hidden, either behind adults or displays on the tables.

Who walked around with shards inside their body?

The power could poison a person as quickly as it could strengthen them, which was why the clan and singers only wore the shards on their bracelets or as jewelry.

Suddenly, his eyes narrowed, and he looked straight at her. She ducked behind the closest pair of adults and risked a quick peek between them. He stared right at her, eyes as hard as steel.

Her opinion of him changed in a heartbeat. He wasn't nearly as oblivious as she'd thought. She imagined walking up to him and introducing herself, but what could she say? He'd caught her spying on him.

Shame flushed her cheeks and she hurried away, back to the nearest stairwell. Though she hadn't been to the surface for more than a few hours, it had taught her much about the opportunities she would have once she'd escaped Father for good. It was a good start for the day, and there would be more opportunities to explore.

Robyn had probably already left to travel to Firestone and Nightkeep, but she'd promised Kaya her door would be open all day. Nothing sounded better than returning there, taking a nice shower, and waiting for the day to end.

Tomorrow, she could try again.

She waited for another group to go down the stairs, then she slipped quietly behind them. As before, the Shield paid her almost no attention at all. Once below, she made her way straight for Robyn's home.

The farther she traveled from the stairwell, the quieter the halls became. When she reached Robyn's door, there wasn't a soul to be seen. She considered knocking but decided to enter without. She twisted the handle and stepped inside, closing the door behind her.

"Robyn?" she asked. She didn't expect an answer, but there was a small chance they would cross paths.

Silence answered, and Kaya was grateful. After being surrounded by people all morning, she wanted nothing more than to have some time to herself. She took her shoes off and started toward the living room, but a smell caught her attention. She sniffed the air. The smell was bitter and slightly metallic, and it came from Robyn's bedroom.

Kaya walked toward the bedroom and poked her head in to make sure everything was fine.

She regretted her curiosity immediately. Parts of Robyn were scattered around, and every surface was covered in blood. Kaya's stomach rebelled as she looked down and saw Robyn's severed hand.

Her thoughts stuttered and skidded to a disbelieving stop. She'd just seen Robyn a few hours ago, so how could this be her? How could any of this have happened?

Before she could answer any of the questions, before the reality of what she saw could break through her shock, footsteps sounded behind her. She tried to turn, but she wasn't quick enough. A dark hood was pulled over her head.

Kaya took a deep breath to scream, only to inhale a sickly-sweet scent that made her head feel light. She stumbled back into strong arms, and then there was nothing at all.

7

———

Radyn looked down at his manacles as though they were part of some dream he had yet to wake up from. Only a few hours ago, he'd been walking through the market with Aria, imagining lives he might someday lead. Now he was in Starfall's mirror image of Firestone's holding cell, and it was like he'd fallen back into his past. He halfway expected Jyn to come striding through the door in a moment.

He'd been in holding cells, what, twice before? Weariness blended the moments together. The first time, they'd thrown a hood over his head. The second had been after the battle that had changed his life for good. Neither were particularly fond memories.

Perhaps his third visit would be his lucky one.

Starfall's holding cells weren't as clean as Firestone's, but that looked to be due more to lack of use than lack of cleaning. Outside of the chair he currently occupied, there was no other furniture. The metal walls were bare.

Dust gathered on the floor, and some spider had spun a beautiful web in one of the upper corners.

The biggest difference between this cell and the one where he and Jyn had met back in Firestone was the door. Firestone's had been thick and metal, but here it had been torn out and replaced with a door of steel bars. He could hear every whisper and creak out in the hallway, but his guards could hear him just as easily.

When he wasn't wondering about his reason for being in the cell, he wondered about that door. Had the Builders created it that way, or had it been replaced by the city at some point?

He didn't know the answer to that any more than he did to the question of why he was imprisoned. At least in Firestone they'd had the good graces to only arrest him after he'd committed crimes.

Purposeful footsteps echoed down the hallway and Radyn figured he'd get his answer soon enough. As near as he could tell, he was the prison's only guest.

The footsteps stopped outside his cell. A thin man in the uniform of a Starfall Shield stood there and stared at Radyn. He had a sharp nose and a mustache that wasn't doing his face any favors. He shifted from side to side stiffly and kept glancing to the side. Radyn had heard multiple pairs of footsteps, but whoever had joined the thin man preferred to stay out of sight.

The Shield didn't bother to introduce himself. "Can you confirm that you are, in fact, Radyn of Firestone, former Sword of your clan?"

"I am." He wanted nothing more than to ask why he

was behind bars, but sensed the man was waiting for just that question, so he kept his lips sealed.

After a moment, the Shield realized Radyn wasn't going to say more and frowned. "Tell me about your day. What did you do?"

"Woke up. Came to the market with my partner. Got arrested. Not too much to say, really."

A slight growl emanated from the back of the Shield's throat. "In detail, please."

"Ahh. Well, my partner and I did stop on the bridge for a while to enjoy the view."

Again, it took the Shield a few moments to realize Radyn wasn't going to say more. He sputtered, then said, "Answer the question!"

"I did."

The Shield's face turned red, and Radyn wondered what he'd attempt if he were physically in the room. He didn't look like he'd last long in a fight, but Radyn had been surprised before. The Shield stepped closer to the bars, almost pressing his face between them. Radyn guessed it was meant to be intimidating, but it ended up making him look silly.

The Shield's next question robbed Radyn of his mirth, though. "Have you killed anybody in the past few days?"

Radyn's eyes narrowed. The Shields up above hadn't been lying. They suspected him of murder. But why? He hadn't so much as swung his fist in anger since he'd been exiled from the clan.

Before he could answer, there was another pair of footsteps in the hallway. These were softer than the ones before, but the Shield who'd been questioning Radyn looked like a child who'd just had their toy taken away. This place was getting crowded, and Radyn still didn't have the slightest idea what was happening.

"Senior Shield, you were specifically told not to conduct this interview until I arrived. You can be certain word of this breach of trust will be reported to your superiors." The voice was a woman's, spoken with the air of someone used to giving orders and having them obeyed.

The Starfall Shield sputtered again, and Radyn wondered if he wouldn't be put to better use up on the surface, watering the crops. "He's a murder suspect! I have every right to interview him."

"He didn't do it. You'll know that for certain the moment you stop wasting my time and checking with merchants up on the surface. He was seen by several people with his partner."

The Shield had no response to that except more sputtering.

"Now, will you open the door so I can speak to him?"

The Shield looked like he might fight the request for a moment, but then he bowed and gestured for the guard standing next to the door to open it. Radyn remained seated, plenty curious about these new developments.

The woman who entered wore the uniform of a Firestone Shield, a deep red. The bars on her shoulder marked her as a Senior Shield, but Radyn didn't think he'd ever crossed paths with her. Her hair was a lighter red than her uniform, and she had a sharp gaze that reminded him of Elora. A thin strap of leather served as a tight necklace. At the front, it held a small ruby.

The Shield bowed to Radyn. It wasn't deep enough to show respect, but enough to be polite. Radyn returned it in kind. "Senior Shield."

"Nikki. I'm here on the personal orders of the Blade."

Radyn sat up straighter. Jyn had always struck him as an excellent judge of a person's character. If she'd been sent personally, it meant something.

What that something was, though, remained unknown. "How can I help you?" he asked.

"As you've no doubt ascertained, a problem has arisen here on Starfall. The Blade fears that, if not taken care of, it may endanger the very peace he's striving for. He has sent me here to request your aid."

Radyn leaned back in his chair. "Why me?"

"He believes, albeit begrudgingly, that you are uniquely suited to help understand what happened here. If you agree, you'd be working with me. It is my hope that by working together, we can bring this case to a swift conclusion."

Radyn's eyes narrowed. He'd believed every word she said up until that last bit. "What part is the lie?"

"Excuse me?"

"The part about us working together, or the part where you claim to want a swift conclusion to the case?"

He'd expected her to push back, to deny the lie. Instead, she grinned. "The working together part. I've always worked alone and didn't see why he'd pair me with a bloodied Sword. But now I'm starting to understand."

Radyn thought for a few moments longer. "Was Jyn involved in the killing?"

Nikki failed to hide the shock on her face. "The Blade would never be involved!"

At the very least, she fully believed in her superior. But that left Radyn in a bind. He considered a bit longer, then shook his head. "I appreciate the offer, but no."

She didn't seem surprised at all, which worried him. "Jyn said you'd refuse. He wanted me to ensure you understood the deal. If you help bring the case to a close, he'll clean the blood from your name. You won't be allowed back into the clan, of course, but you won't have to watch your back every minute of the day."

"And if I don't?"

"Then you'll be left here. As you can tell, there's a Senior Shield here who very much believes you're responsible for a murder, and no one besides Jyn and Aria is going to fight for your release. If Starfall wants you to sit in their cells for a few days or weeks, what does that matter?"

"How is Aria?" Radyn asked.

"She's worried about you. She went to the academy and tried to barge her way in but was stopped by a pair of Daggers. Now she's haunting the central neighborhood, arguing with every Shield who steps foot out of headquarters. For now, she's fine, but if she's not careful, she's going to get arrested for being a nuisance."

Radyn fixed his gaze on Nikki. "Threaten me all you want, but walk very carefully when you talk about Aria."

Nikki held up her hands, not in mock surrender, but a genuine gesture of peace. Even though he was manacled, she took his warning seriously. She grimaced. "Sorry, that was a poor choice of words. All I meant to say is that she's safe and doing everything she can to get you released, even though it won't amount to anything."

Radyn gave Nikki a short bow. "Thank you."

He stared up at the ceiling as he thought. The choice was an obvious one, but he hated the feeling of being jerked around by Jyn. He didn't owe the Blade a damned thing, and now he had the gall to send this Shield here, thinking he could coerce Radyn into doing his dirty work. It stank worse than a pig pen.

He couldn't deny its effectiveness, though. Jyn knew he had no desire to rejoin the clan, but wiping the blood from his name would be a very public welcoming back into the fold. Aria wouldn't have to suffer as an outcast for Radyn's actions any longer. That alone probably made the deal worth it.

"Why is Jyn going to all this trouble for a murder, especially one here? I get they're not that common, and the timing couldn't be worse, but there has to be more than that if he's reaching out to me."

Nikki shrugged, but Radyn couldn't tell if that was because she didn't know the answer or she didn't want to share it. "Jyn told me that we needed to solve this case to help Firestone. That was all I needed to know."

Radyn's answering laugh was bitter. "If that was his only reason, you can forget it."

She looked as surprised by that as she had his question about whether Jyn was involved. "You hate your own city so much?"

Radyn snorted. He knew he was treading on thin

ground, but he said, "I tried to save my city once, and see where it got me? No, I don't think I'm that interested in trying again."

Nikki looked at him for a moment, and he got the sense she was trying to understand him. He leaned back and let her look, and a smile came across her face. "That all may be true, but you're forgetting something."

"What's that?"

"This time, you'll be working with me."

Radyn stared at her, trying to decide if she'd made a joke or not. He really didn't know. "Are you saying that you're good?"

"What do you think?" she asked.

"As much as Jyn and I don't get along, he knows his people well. If he orders you about personally, it's for a reason."

She inclined her head. "I'm the best Shield in Firestone, at least in regards to solving unique problems. As you yourself said, there's a reason why the Blade summoned me."

Radyn reached up with both his hands and scratched an itch at the back of his neck. He cursed Jyn silently. It had been less than a year since he'd endured the public humiliation that resulted from his last attempt to save Firestone. A wise man, sitting in Radyn's place, would run away from Nikki as fast as his feet would carry him.

But honestly, he liked Nikki. She seemed clever, decisive, and confident. She was offering him the opportunity to use the skills Elora had given him, something that farming, for all its usefulness, never did.

And it would make life easier for both him and Aria. Mostly Aria.

He swore out loud, cursing Jyn's name to eternal torment. The Blade had likely never been in doubt of the outcome.

He held out his manacled hands. "Fine. It sounds to me like you have a new partner."

8

———

Radyn gently rubbed his hands where the manacles had bit at his wrists. They hadn't been on so tight as to be painful, but he still imagined them around his wrists. No doubt, had it been up to Starfall's Shields, he'd still be in the cell. The Senior Shield had been furious about Nikki's arrangement, but it had all been decided by authorities far above his head. He had his orders, and he had little choice but to let Radyn walk free.

The Shield had, of course, threatened to scrutinize every step Radyn took within his city. Given the man's clear dislike of him, Radyn didn't have any problem believing the threat, nor was he concerned by it. He didn't plan to remain long. Once he'd fulfilled his duty toward Jyn's lapdog, he'd find Aria and not leave their home until the other cities had flown far away.

Thinking of Aria lightened his mood. Nikki assured him she was safe back in Firestone, and Radyn believed her. He'd check once he returned, but Starfall's ire had been focused exclusively on him. When he returned, he had little doubt she'd make fun of his inability to travel to another city without causing trouble.

He gently swept aside thoughts of Aria. Few people distracted him like she did, and he wanted the full extent of his faculties available. Nikki led him upstairs and around corners without slowing.

"You know this city well," he observed.

The ponytail at the back of her neck shook side to side. "Same design as Firestone. I know whose apartment it would be back home, so I just have to find it here."

Radyn grunted. "Do you know where everyone lives in Firestone?"

"No, but most. And before you ask to test me, you live at 221 Blue section, Level 12."

"I wasn't going to ask you where I lived."

Her answer came without hesitation. She hadn't so much as glanced back at him. "Yes, you were."

Her confidence elicited a low chuckle. "Yeah, maybe I was. I'm impressed, though I suppose I should be if Jyn has you at his beck and call."

He'd hoped to get a rise out of her, but she acted as though she hadn't heard him. They stopped at a door and Nikki spared him her first glance. "I realize you're a Sword that's seen plenty of battle, but I've heard the scene within is gruesome. You ready?"

Radyn nodded and she opened the door, startling two Starfall Shields on the other side. "You can't be in here," said a broad-shouldered, thick-chested man. His insignia marked him as the higher ranked of the two Shields. The Shield tried to cross his arms, but they were so thick it was more like he rested one on top of the other.

Many Shields were people who had attempted to join their clan and failed at some point in the grueling training. Radyn guessed he was looking at one such man. If he had to guess further, the man had been unable to connect with shards. To attempt to compensate, he'd developed his body as far as it would go. He would have failed the trials, though, as control over the shards was a vital aspect of becoming a Dagger. He now carried a grudge, and he would be thrilled to wield his meager influence over citizens who had even less than him.

Radyn and Nikki both bowed deeper than necessary. He was surprised she joined him. He'd grown used to acting demure over the past months, but there was no reason for her to show such respect. She had every right to be here.

While holding the bow, she extended her orders, bearing Jyn's seal. "Apologies. My Blade has spoken with yours and has given me permission to launch my own investigation."

A growl escaped the back of the massive Shield's throat. "We don't need your help."

"I agree. I have no doubt you'll be up to the task. But my Blade is concerned, given the identity of the victim, and wishes to appear involved."

The Starfall Shield grunted and threw Nikki's orders back at her. Radyn noticed how her hand flicked out to easily catch the falling paper. Her head was still bowed.

The Shield continued, "Name's Rolph. I'm the one who's going to solve this case. I don't mind if you want to tag along and watch, but if you interfere, I'll boot you off this city, and it won't be back across the bridge, if you catch my meaning." The massive Shield waved a dismissive hand at them. "Look around if you want, but there's nothing here that tells us who the killer is."

Nikki bowed a fraction deeper before rising. She looked past Rolph and his partner and around the room. Radyn did the same. The smell of blood was heavy in the air, mixed with a cloying sweet scent he couldn't place. Otherwise, the living room appeared undisturbed. Radyn noted the pillow and the blankets on the couch, but his attention was drawn to the drawings hanging in the corner.

He walked over and examined them. Most were of a young woman, though in some, a young man accompanied her. They were well done, with smooth and confident strokes. The drawings were more realistic and less stylized than most Radyn had seen, but Radyn appreciated them. These were closer to something true, but he felt the artist trying to express something deeper, even as he worked within tight constraints.

Radyn nodded toward the drawings. "Did the victim create these?"

Rolph made a face that made Radyn wonder if the question caused him physical pain. "Not sure. All I know right now is that she was a cook for the nearby kitchens. I plan to question them after the recyclers come for the body."

Nikki stood beside Radyn and joined him in his examination. "These are incredible."

"I was thinking the same."

Rolph grunted. "I'm not sure how you all investigate in Firestone, but the crime happened in the bedroom, not in the drawings."

Radyn caught a slight tightening of Nikki's lips at Rolph's provocation, but it only lasted for a moment, then she turned and bowed toward him. "Of course."

He followed her from the living room, but they didn't make it far before they stopped. Nikki stood, rooted in place just outside the door to the bedroom. Radyn stepped to the side so he could look in, too. His stomach dropped at the sight.

He sometimes forgot how much blood the human body contained, and this bedroom had been decorated with what appeared to be every drop from two victims. Pools of blood had formed around the bodies, but there were smaller puddles where severed limbs lay detached from their proper torsos.

Radyn had seen violent fights, but nothing like this. A battle was always terrible, but it was constrained. Warriors fought to kill one another in pursuit of a larger objective. Right or wrong, Radyn understood it.

He couldn't wrap his head around this. The first victim he focused on was an older woman. Though she had aged since the drawings had been made, the face was still recognizably the one sketched so many times out in the living room. The resident of the apartment, then.

He looked to Nikki. Given how quickly she'd frozen at the sight, he expected to see her in a state of shock. He could hardly blame her, as he had to fight off the feeling, too. Except she had never been frozen. He saw now that she had only stopped to examine the room before entering it. Her gaze flicked from place to place, resting on each gruesome sight for as long as she felt she needed.

He grunted softly to himself. An impressive woman.

He took his cue from her and returned his gaze to the bloody bedroom. "Do you mind if I step in?" he asked.

Nikki held up a hand for a minute, then let it drop. "Sure. Let's not move more than we have to, though."

Radyn stepped in, careful to place his feet in places where blood hadn't pooled. He went first to the woman. It was clear she'd died hard. Given the amount of blood around her limbs and around her wounds, it appeared that most of her injuries had taken place before she'd died. His stomach clenched, and for a moment, he feared he would be sick.

In a proper fight, death was delivered as quickly as possible. It wasn't always as quick as it should have been, but the intent was there. This had been slow and intentionally so. Why? Either someone had really hated her, or there'd been another reason to inflict this pain.

At least one fact was clear: the wounds had been caused by a maniblade. Nothing else cut through flesh so cleanly.

Radyn stepped back from the parts of the body, taking one last look at the entire scene. She'd been killed slowly, losing one limb at a time. He examined her detached hands more closely but saw no blood under the fingernails. There were no bruises on her body that he could see.

When he'd learned all from the body that he could, he allowed himself to look at the second body. This one wasn't in nearly as gruesome condition as the first. It only displayed one wound, a deep cut that ran along the back of his neck, severing the spine and almost cutting the head off completely.

Like the first, the wound had been caused by a maniblade. Radyn bent down and examined the cut closer. It appeared to have been made by a skilled hand. The cut had come straight across, and Radyn detected no difference in depth or width—a clean strike.

But if it had been made by someone skilled, why didn't they cut all the way through the head? Assuming the criminal was clan, they were trained to take the whole head with their cuts. It was the most certain way of killing an enemy, and a maniblade didn't have to worry about getting stuck between vertebrae.

He was even more surprised when he turned the second body's face so he could see it. He started. "I know him."

"Josiah. A Dagger of Firestone's clan," Nikki said.

Radyn looked up at her, trying to find a calm center among the turbulent emotions raging through his chest. Some of the pieces of the mystery fell into place. He didn't have the slightest clue what had happened in this bedroom, but he finally understood why he was here.

Only the sound of Rolph's heavy breathing in the next room kept him from unleashing his full displeasure upon Nikki. She met his gaze without flinching away. She'd known before they had entered the room.

He closed his eyes. He might be furious, but it didn't change anything. He'd made the agreement with her, knowing full well there was more to the story than Nikki had told him, and he didn't doubt Starfall's Senior

Shield would be more than happy to throw him back into a cell.

Jyn might be a scoundrel, but Radyn trusted the Blade to keep the letter of his word. He forced himself to take a deep, slow breath. Tension drained from his shoulders, and when he opened his eyes again, his thoughts were clear.

Josiah hadn't been wearing his uniform, but he wore the clip at his hip where a maniblade would have been carried. The clip was empty, and though Radyn searched the entire room, he didn't find one.

His gaze fell to Josiah's arms and hands. They were bloody, but when Radyn grabbed his wrist and twisted so that he could see Josiah's palms, they were reasonably clean.

His throat constricted. Josiah had been younger than him, a part of a different group of initiates, but he'd seemed a good man. He'd been committed to defending Firestone, just like them all.

Radyn felt sick, and it had nothing to do with the scene before him but what he was increasingly certain the scene represented. He stood and wandered around the room. He peeked under the bed and looked through the dresser quickly. No maniblades had been hidden in the room, and as near as he could tell, the woman who had lived here had enjoyed a peaceable life. He saw nothing that led him to believe she was anything more than she appeared, but he didn't rule it out, either.

Elora had always cautioned him against judging too quickly. Even if he was right, it narrowed his vision. Once he started to create a story, it took him one more step away from reality.

He stepped back out into the living room, where Rolph and his companion were eagerly waiting for Radyn and Nikki to finish. "Did you find any maniblades?" Radyn asked.

Rolph shook his head.

Radyn wasn't sure Rolph knew the answer to his next question, but if his guess of the man's history was correct, he would. "Are clan warriors here taught to take the head of an opponent in a fight, or do they have a different technique?"

Rolph's gaze hardened. "Why do you want to know?"

There didn't seem to be any benefit in lying. They were supposed to be working together, after all. Radyn gestured back to the bedroom. "The second victim died from a clean cut. A skilled warrior, most likely. I'm confused as to why the murderer didn't just take his head. In Firestone, clan teaching is to cut through the entire neck. If your clan is trained to do differently, it would mean it's more likely one of your clan did this instead of one of ours."

Rolph bristled. "There's no chance one of our clan did this."

Radyn didn't bother to argue. Nothing he said would make a difference. "Are they trained to take the head?"

Rolph took two threatening steps toward Radyn, only stopping once he towered over Radyn. "Yes, they're trained to take the head."

Radyn was tempted to bow, but if he did, he'd bump into Rolph's crossed arms. "Thank you."

Nikki came out of the bedroom a moment later. "Have you seen everything you need?" she asked Radyn.

Radyn looked once more around the room. He caught a detail near the door he'd missed, thanks to their first confrontation with Rolph. A small pair of shoes rested on the mat.

"I think I have, thank you," he told Nikki.

"Then let's get out of here before we waste any more of Rolph's time," she said.

"And just where do you two think you're going after this?" Rolph asked.

Nikki answered for both of them. "I haven't decided yet, but if we learn anything important, you can be sure that we'll let you know. Do you have any idea who might have been behind this?"

Rolph grunted. "I've got some theories, but I'll need to speak to some people to see if any of them have teeth."

The Shield was a terrible liar. He was lost without a clue but too proud to admit it.

Radyn and Nikki bowed and exited, and Radyn was glad Rolph didn't try to follow them. He had some hard questions for Nikki, and it was best he ask them someplace where they wouldn't be overheard.

9

───────

Radyn waited until they were well away from the scene to confront Nikki. He glanced behind to ensure any curious Shields weren't following them and wasn't surprised to see their stretch of hallway was empty besides them. Thanks to the pull of the Gathering on the surface, these residential hallways might as well be abandoned. Once he was certain they were alone, he stopped.

She noticed so quickly he wondered if she'd anticipated him. She turned and waited for him to unleash his anger and questions.

He didn't disappoint her. "You tricked me!"

"You knew perfectly well there was more to this than I told you in the cell."

"Did Jyn tell you why he sent a Dagger to kill a cook in Starfall, or did that slip his mind?"

Nikki's nostrils flared. She tamped down the reaction quickly, but she didn't like it when he insinuated that the Blade was guilty of anything more criminal than being late to a council meeting. That was the lever he'd have to pull if he needed an emotional reaction from her.

She took a few seconds to visibly master her temper, making him wait for an answer. The corner of her mouth eventually turned up in a smile. "I can see why Jyn recommended you. Not many would have figured out the second victim was the first victim's killer."

"Blood up and down his arms, but his palms were reasonably clean. He was using a maniblade to carve her up like she was a roasted pig in her own kitchen." He waved his observations away, letting her know he considered them nothing special. "Did you know before you stepped into the room?"

To her credit, she didn't dissemble any further. "No. When Jyn summoned me this afternoon, he told me a Firestone Dagger had been found dead at a murder scene in Starfall. He told me to get your help. That was all I knew."

Radyn didn't notice any hint of a lie, but his trust in her was as thin as silk. "The timing doesn't make sense, either. The murders happened this morning. The bodies couldn't even have been cold by the time I was arrested."

Radyn ran his best guess at timing through his head. The pair had been murdered sometime that morning. Their bodies were stiffening but hadn't completely, which meant they'd only been dead a handful of hours at most. If everything had happened without coincidence or conspiracy, it meant the bodies had been found bare minutes after they'd dropped, and he'd been arrested less than an hour later. Jyn would have had to have found out about his imprisonment quickly, too.

It could work, he supposed, but it assumed too much. Something had sped the process along.

He pushed the problem aside. He couldn't solve it yet, but a bigger problem stood right in front of him. "The only reason Jyn wants me here is because he thinks something is happening in the clan, and I'm a convenient tool to weed it out. Otherwise, he wouldn't have come anywhere near me with this."

Radyn expected Nikki to deny it, so he was surprised when she agreed. "That was my thought as well. A clever maneuver on his part. Not only do you have the aptitude for such a task, but both of us stand outside the clan. He loses no face by having us poking around, and he can deny any involvement if the need arises."

"That paper you carry says otherwise."

"Nonsense. If it gets brought up, I'll destroy it and, if pressed, claim that I forged it."

Radyn's jaw moved, but no words came out for a solid minute. "You're that loyal to him?"

"He's the Blade of Firestone. Aren't you?"

Her eyes glanced to the side for a moment, but Radyn didn't press. He didn't need to know why. Simply knowing her feelings was enough.

He shook his head. "I can't be involved in this. This is a clan problem. If anyone finds out I'm investigating, they'll form their maniblades and chase me until I'm dead at their feet."

"Your Blade has asked for your help." Nikki's voice became harsher than he'd heard from her before. "You have a duty to help him and Firestone."

Radyn was in her face before he was consciously

aware of it. She was a bit taller than him, but he tried to stare her down anyway. "No! I don't owe Firestone a damn thing, and I owe Jyn even less."

Nikki wasn't even flustered. Her sharp eyes bore into him like needles. "Interesting. You think you'd feel differently, given that it was your foolishness that got Nuela killed and almost doomed Firestone to destruction."

Radyn sealed his lips and pressed them hard together. He cursed his own impulsiveness. She'd turned the momentum of the conversation against him, making him too emotional to protect Jyn's secrets. He stepped back and forced his breath through his nose until he was calm enough to unclench his fists. Her gaze never left him.

For a long minute, they stood and stared at one another.

Nikki broke the stalemate. Her voice was soft. "That was rude of me. I'll confess that I'm curious. The Blade is welcome to his secrets, and it's clear to me that you're one of them. I do not have the Blade's complete confidence, but I know him well. I do not believe he is playing you falsely. I think you are correct that he wants your help because of the difficulties he faces with factions of Firestone's clan, but there is nothing personal in the decision. You are the perfect tool for the problem at hand."

"It's personal for me. It's my neck at risk."

"And I'm more than happy to help you as best I can. I can act as your Shield in dealings with clan, but I believe the Blade judged well when he suggested I seek your help."

Radyn put his hands on his hips and stared at her. "You're not going to try coercing me by saying that if I don't cooperate, you'll let the clan know that I was already involved at the crime scene?"

That hint of a smile returned. "The idea occurred to me, but I don't want to coerce you. If you are going to help, I'd have it be your choice."

"But if I refuse, you'll still hand me back to Starfall's Shields?"

"Unfortunately, yes. Those were the Blade's explicit orders."

Radyn rubbed his eyes. This was getting to be a long day. "Fine. You win. Where do you want to start?"

"Being as we're here, I'd planned on the kitchens. I want to know what child was staying with her."

Despite himself, Radyn grunted, impressed again. "You figured that out, too?"

"Shoes, made-up couch, and no drawings of a young girl to be found. Nothing conclusive, but I don't believe she had children."

Radyn nodded. Her thoughts matched his exactly. His heart beat a little faster and he looked forward to asking around the kitchen about the victim.

He wasn't sure how Aria was going to take all the news when he finally related it to her, but he had to admit he was excited.

It was the first time he'd felt truly alive since the day Nightkeep had attacked.

∾

The kitchen was as busy a place as Radyn had ever seen. Having never been privy to the massive operations required to feed a city, he watched in amazement as chefs danced around one another, working over the open flames to prepare meals for hundreds. The longer he watched, the more convinced he became that clan commanders could learn something from observing the controlled chaos.

Every chef was in constant motion. A single person might be supervising a stove while chopping onions for a dish not yet started. They possessed perfect awareness of their surroundings, shifting subtly as other chefs passed behind them with enormous pots of boiling stew. Sweat poured from faces, but Radyn thought he sensed satisfaction running underneath every action. It was hard work but good work, which made a meaningful contribution to others.

He and Nikki sat in the dining room across from the head chef for this kitchen, who was anything but satisfied at the news that one of his treasured cooks had died. He had his hat in his hands and kept shaking his head as if doing so would make their words less true.

"You say she was murdered?" he asked.

His name was Karl, and his hands were as calloused and wounded as a veteran Sword's.

Nikki nodded. "I'm sorry to be the one to tell you."

"Who would do such a thing? Robyn was one of the kindest souls I've ever worked with," Karl said.

"That's what we're going to find out," Nikki assured him. "Right now, we don't know much about her, and we were hoping you could tell us what she was like."

Karl wiped the tears away from his eyes. At first, Radyn had thought the chef's reaction a bit strong, but the longer he spent with the man, the more convinced he became it was simply the man's way. This kitchen was his home, and his cooks his family.

"She truly was one of the kindest people. That's no exaggeration. She'd often work late at night to take food to people who couldn't make it to the kitchens for a meal. Volunteered to do it more nights than not."

"When we were in her home, we saw a number of drawings of her and a man. Was she married?"

"Was, yes. Her husband was an artist, but he passed through the gates several years ago. He got caught by an illness the healers couldn't stay in front of. He was probably the only person I've ever met kinder than her. All of us were devastated at his passing."

"Did they have any children?" Nikki asked.

"No, and I think that was one of Robyn's greatest regrets. I hadn't known her that long at the time her husband passed, but I'm pretty sure they tried for years, but it never worked. She had an enormous soft spot for children, though. She snuck more sweets into more meals than anyone else in the kitchen, that's for sure."

While Nikki chewed on the chef's answers, Radyn asked, "When we were in her apartment, it looked like she had a guest staying with her. Did she tell you anything about that?"

Karl shook his head. "No, but it's not as though I talk to everyone every day. We've been busting our tails to keep up with all the demands of the Gathering." He paused and narrowed his eyes. "Although her station was surprisingly low on food yesterday. I was going to ask her about it when I got the chance. I thought maybe she'd delivered some meals and had forgotten to record them."

Nikki took over the interview. "You've been a tremendous help, and we don't want to take any more of your time than we need. Is there anyone you could think that we should talk to about Robyn?"

Karl gave them an apologetic shrug. "You're welcome to talk to anyone in the kitchen, of course, but I don't know that anyone will be able to tell you much more than I can. She was friendly and kind but not close to others. It always felt like she kept people at arm's length after her husband passed away."

"Is there any reason you can think of that someone would want to harm her?"

A look of anguish passed over Karl's face. "It's all I've been asking myself since you told me, but I can't think of a thing. She was about the last person in this kitchen I would expect to come to harm. I'm sorry I can't help you more."

Nikki stood and Radyn followed her lead. "No, it's me that's sorry. She sounds like she was a wonderful woman. I wish I could do more, but for now, all I can do is promise I will do everything in my power to find and punish whoever did this."

Karl bowed his head in thanks, but his thoughts were somewhere else as Radyn and Nikki took their leave.

Once they were outside the kitchen door, Radyn said, "Josiah most likely killed her. Why not tell him her killer is dead?"

"'Most likely' isn't good enough. There are other,

albeit more implausible, explanations that could work. I want to know. And even though I agree it was most likely Josiah, we still don't have the slightest idea why a Firestone Dagger tortured and killed an old widow in Starfall. It's not a true answer, not yet."

Radyn yawned. It was nearing time for the evening meal, but he felt as though he'd been awake for several days straight. "The missing food is interesting, don't you think?"

Nikki agreed. "It could have been a mistake, but it seems more likely she was bringing food to her guest."

"Why would she do that? If someone was hungry, they could just go to the dining room and eat at every meal. There's no reason to ever go hungry on a city."

Nikki followed his thoughts easily. "Unless Robyn's guest was hiding."

"But why? If I knew someone was looking for me, I'd just go to a different dining room."

"Not if the whole city is looking for you. Maybe Robyn was sheltering a criminal and knew it. Maybe Josiah was part of some criminal gang, and that was what got Robyn killed."

It sounded thin, but he didn't have any better ideas. "If we assume that's true, how should we proceed?"

Nikki grimaced as though she'd just eaten something bitter. "I think we reach out to the Shields to see if there's been any noticeable criminal activity lately. That might give us something to latch onto."

Radyn nodded. "Then let's go pay a visit to some of our favorite Shields. I'm sure they'll be delighted to see us."

10

Kaya returned to consciousness slowly, sleep clinging to her like a desperate friend. The sweet smell of the hood lingered in her nose, even though the hood itself had been removed. She shoved herself away from the dreams that begged her to return. She cracked an eye open and groaned.

A light across the room dimly glowed, and though it was set low, the light pierced her eye like a spear. Her head pounded in tandem with her heart and she squeezed her eyes tightly shut.

The effects of whatever she'd inhaled kept most of her fear at bay, sanding away its sharp edges until all that remained was mild concern. She remembered the sight of Robyn's bedroom. Some sights, she was sure, burned themselves so deep into memories they never faded. Then there had been the hood and now she was here.

She felt as though she wandered in a dream, as though the world was nothing but a nightmare that refused to release her. She'd long believed something similar, but never more than at this moment. Only the Song was real.

She heard it even now. It was a different key than the Song that had greeted her every morning at home, but it was the same Song.

She cracked open her eyes, lifting her hand up in front of her face to block some of the light from the lamp. Her eyes adjusted and she took in her new surroundings.

She lay in a bed, the covers tucked over her. The lamp had been turned down low and a cup of water rested on the nightstand. Her throat was dry, so she grabbed the cup and took a sip. The water was cool but lacked the slightly metallic tang she associated with Nightkeep water. It tasted like Starfall water.

She sat fully up and shoved the covers off her. She was still in her clothes, and she wondered if they had remembered to grab her shoes.

Kaya shook her head. She'd been taken by the same person who'd killed Robyn. Her shoes were likely the least of her worries. She blamed the smelly substance in the hood. Even now, her thoughts crawled sluggishly and her emotions were muted. Under other circumstances, she was certain she'd be pounding at the door, screaming to be let out.

Instead, she looked around the room again. It was as plain as a room as she'd ever visited. Nothing hung on the wall. There was only a bed, a nightstand, and a dresser, and the nightstand was empty except for the cup of water. Still, she was in a room, which was more than she would have expected.

She swung her legs out of the bed and tested her

weight on them. They seemed strong, so she tried standing. She passed that test, and though her balance was slightly wobbly, she padded over to the dresser. She tugged on a drawer, and it smoothly slid out. Like the nightstand, it was empty.

Voices trickled under the crack in the door, too softly to make out the words. The mood seemed tense, though.

Kaya looked around the room. There were no other exits, and kidnappers and killers waited on the other side. She would have to escape, but the time wasn't yet. The drug they'd given her stole too much of the concentration she'd need. Once it wore off, though, she'd fight her way through them.

She didn't consider herself equal to the clans, but Father had insisted she go through some basic training. She suspected it had more to do with him wanting to see if her gift helped her in combat than it did with him wanting to make sure she could protect herself, but the result was the same. If her guards were merely citizens, she might escape them with ease.

For now, she returned to the bed to lie down. The headache had faded with some movement, but it still pressed against the backs of her eyes. Her movements remained sluggish. She'd likely only have one good chance to escape, and there was no point wasting it in this condition.

Time lost meaning in the room. She didn't sleep, but she wasn't alert, either. Her mind drifted along the currents of the Song, which eased the worst of her worries. Whatever happened, life would turn out the way it was supposed to. The Song continued, regardless of what happened to her. It was all as it should be.

Or was it?

The question sent her thoughts in a downward spiral. What had happened to Robyn should never have happened to anyone, and now she'd been captured by the criminals who'd murdered a kindhearted cook. As the drugs wore off, she held herself tight, though it did little to reassure her.

The soft knock on her door made her bolt straight upright. Her thoughts still felt slower than usual, but her time of recuperation had come to an end.

"May I come in?"

The gentle voice and polite question jarred against Kaya's expectations. The voice waited a minute, then the door cracked open. A woman, older than Father but younger than Robyn, poked her head in. When she saw Kaya up, she bowed deeply. "Ah, good, you're awake. I was hoping we might talk, if you were feeling up to it."

Kaya struggled to make sense of the encounter. Robyn's gruesome murder and her kidnapping didn't match with her being tucked into this comfortable bed and left to sleep. And the door had opened without the woman having to unlock it.

Was she even a prisoner?

Her captor didn't seem dismayed by her lack of response. She opened the door a bit wider so she could step in. "I'm sure this is all very confusing and disorienting. Soon, I will hopefully have time to explain everything, but I'm afraid time is growing short, and I have some very important questions to ask."

She stepped deeper into the room and Kaya scrambled as far away as she could. It was only a few inches, but she pressed her back against the wall and clutched her blankets tight.

The woman stopped and her eyes went wide. She held up her hands. "Oh, I'm very sorry. I didn't mean to worry you. We don't want any harm to come to you."

Kaya looked to the open door and wondered if she could get around the woman. She didn't appear intimidating, but some of the most dangerous Swords on Nightkeep could say the same.

On the other hand, the woman hadn't done anything to her since Kaya had woken up.

"What do you want?" Kaya asked.

"I just want to ask you some questions."

"What kind of questions?"

The woman bit her lower lip as she thought. "I suppose first I'd want to know if you're the young lady the Shields have been looking for. The one who appeared in the Engine room several days ago."

Kaya's first instinct was to lie, but she reconsidered. The woman had to know she was. Otherwise, why would Kaya be here in the first place? She gave her head one quick nod.

Her captor's eyes brightened. "And how exactly did you come to be in the Engine room?"

Could she trust her captor? After what she and her people had done to Robyn, she didn't think she could. The knowledge of her gifts had twisted her father, the one person left in the world who was supposed to protect her. What would that knowledge do a stranger already more than willing to kill?

"I was playing hide and seek with some friends."

The light in the woman's gaze died, but Kaya didn't think it was because the woman believed her.

Before she could ask her next question, there was a knock at the door to the apartment Kaya's prison was a part of. The knock sounded again, sounding a pattern that eased some of the sudden tension in her captor's shoulders. The door was opened and there was a quick, hushed conversation in the living room. Even with the door open, Kaya couldn't hear the words, but the tone was hurried and nervous.

Her captor's eyes darted between the open door and Kaya.

After a minute, a tall man entered the room. He had to duck to make sure his head didn't strike the door frame. He looked between the two women, then said, "We've got a problem. It's hard to be sure, but I think the net is drawing tight. We'll need to move soon."

"How much time do we have?" the woman asked.

"If it was up to me alone, I'd say none. We should be leaving now."

"I haven't even confirmed it's her yet."

"Your problem to solve. I'll get us packed." The man left the room in a rush, his long strides carrying him out of sight in a moment.

The woman put her hands on her hips. "I need you to tell me what you can do. Otherwise, I'm not sure how I can help you."

Kaya kept her lips sealed. This woman didn't want to

help her any more than Father did. If she was lucky, the rest of them would leave and she would be left here to fend for herself.

The woman pursed her lips and exhaled sharply through her nose. Finally, she said, "Fine. Be that way." She stomped out of the room and there was another hurried conversation.

Kaya stood and inched toward the door.

The woman reappeared before Kaya got close to the door. The tall man and a bulkier man followed her in. Kaya's heart began to pound hard against her chest. She backed up a step. The bulkier man had a dark hood stretched between his hands, and Kaya smelled that same sweet odor. It made her stomach twist.

"No!" Kaya shouted as the woman gestured.

She had no shards, but the Song gave her strength, and she sprinted for the door.

The bulkier man moved faster than he should have, and the hood snapped closed over her head. She held her breath and tried to run, but the man's grip was firm. A long pair of arms wrapped around her in an awkward embrace, pinning her arms to her sides.

She struggled, but she couldn't hold her breath for long. Eventually, she had to inhale. Strength fled her limbs and the grip around her arms loosened. She sensed movement but couldn't tell which direction was up.

The last thing she heard was the woman's voice.

"Don't take it off. She's going to need to sleep for a while now."

11

Radyn followed Nikki through the hallways, feeling a bit like a child being led around by their parent. When they'd decided to speak to the Shields, he'd assumed they would head straight for Starfall's headquarters, but Nikki argued they'd have better luck at one of the local outposts scattered throughout the city. Radyn took her word for it, grateful she knew where the closest one would be located.

A handful of twists, turns, and stairs led them to a door with the symbols for "Shield" inscribed upon it. Nikki opened the door without knocking and barged in. Within was a single small room with a handful of desks scattered about. It looked cramped and unpleasant, as though designed to encourage the Shields to be on their feet and patrolling the hallways. At that moment, only one desk was occupied, and the Shield sitting behind the desk was Rolph. He looked up at their sudden intrusion.

The change that came over his face was almost

comical in its intensity. He looked ready to exile them to the nearest prison settlement that minute. "What are you two doing here?"

"Have there been any thieves or criminals in this neighborhood, or even adjoining neighborhoods, lately?" Nikki asked.

Having his question ignored nearly tipped Rolph over the edge into violence. He stood so fast his chair went flying backward and he slammed his hands on his desk. Radyn felt the violence of the blow through the soles of his feet. He was surprised the desk survived the assault.

"You do not get to come in here and order me around as though you own the place! You're guests here, and barely welcome ones at that."

Nikki held up her hands for peace. "And this will help! We have reason to believe that Robyn might have been protecting someone or hiding them. We suspect that it was a criminal, so we're wondering what kinds of crime you've experienced lately or if there's a thief you've been tracking. This might be just the lead we've been looking for."

The answer mollified Rolph, but only a little. He crossed his thick arms. "We don't have much crime here, and there's been nothing notable as of late, except the murder."

Nikki's back and forth with the Starfall Shield continued, but Radyn paid their discussion little attention. Rolph wouldn't know anything. He looked around the room, and his eyes stopped on a piece of paper sitting on a neighboring desk. It had a sketch of a girl who looked familiar, but it took him a moment to place the face.

It was the girl from the Gathering, the one who had been following him around. He stepped toward the desk and picked up the piece of paper.

It made him the new center of Rolph's attention. "Just what do you think you're doing?"

Radyn held up the piece of paper. "This girl. Why are you looking for her?"

"I don't know. It's a clan matter. They've got every Shield in the city looking for her, but she hasn't shown her dirty face yet. Now, put that down. You two can't come in here and act like you own the place."

Radyn bowed to Rolph and turned on his heel. Nikki frowned but followed him, leaving Rolph speechless and alone.

Once they were in the hallway and Radyn was certain Rolph wasn't going to follow them, he said, "Robyn was sheltering the girl, and now she's missing."

Nikki tracked his thoughts without a problem. "So, this wasn't about Robyn. It was about the girl."

Radyn nodded. "But we've gone as far as we can for now unless you think you can make any progress with Starfall's clan."

Nikki shook her head. "I'll need to speak to the Blade. He's not going to be happy."

"You'll have to tell me how it goes."

"Oh, no. If you think you can leave my side now, you're going to be very disappointed."

"There's nothing I can do to help you on Firestone.

Not only will you want to talk to Jyn, but you'll need to dig deeper into Josiah's past, and I can't be anywhere near the clan. You don't need to worry about me, though. All I'm going to do is go home, visit with Aria, and maybe get some rest. I'll be waiting there whenever you need me."

"Or you can come with me, and we don't have to have this fight."

"If you try bringing me anywhere close to the academy, you'll have a fight on your hands with at least a half dozen angry Daggers."

He could sense the gears turning in her head. She knew he was right, but she was nervous about him being free. Finally, she nodded. "Deal."

He nodded. "Good. Now, can we please get off this city before Rolph comes up with a new reason to arrest me?"

Radyn hadn't believed it was possible. For nearly a year, daily existence within Firestone had felt like walking through a battlefield, expecting a deadly confrontation every time he turned a corner. But the minute he was across the bridge and back in Firestone, the weight of the last day fell from his shoulders. He almost looked forward to the sneers and angry stares. He ignored the pointed looks of a pair of Daggers wandering over the bridge to enjoy Starfall's evening festivities and hurried home without delay.

He opened the door and grinned. "Aria, I'm home!"

He'd expected to find her on the couch reading. It was her favorite pastime and where she almost always rested after a long day in the shop. When he didn't see her there, he first assumed that she was still out bargaining for his release, but then he heard footsteps in the bedroom.

He took off his shoes and walked that way. "Aria?'

"One minute," she called, and there was a tremor in her voice. He hurried the last few steps to the bedroom and looked in. Aria sat on the edge of the bed, head in her hands.

Radyn rushed over and knelt before her. "What's wrong?"

She didn't answer, but she pulled her hair behind her ears and looked at him.

Her left eye was almost swollen shut. The bruise traveled from her forehead down to her cheek. His shock only lasted a moment before red-tinged the edges of his vision. He connected with the shards buried in his body and brought them to life. The exhaustion and hunger that had been at the forefront of his thoughts faded away like fog dissipating in the bright morning sun.

"Who did this?"

It didn't matter who she named. If she told him Jyn was responsible, he'd kill the Blade without a second thought.

She shook her head. "I don't know. I didn't recognize them. They moved too fast to be civilian, though. I'm sure they were clan."

"What happened?"

She wiped her nose with a handkerchief. It came

away with both snot and dried blood. "Once you were arrested, I went straight to the academy."

Radyn's heart pounded faster. He knew it was only his name that had been blooded, but to know she'd braved the academy made him ashamed. An overeager Dagger might have hurt her to get to him, and if they did, her injuries would look a lot like this. He forced himself to listen, though.

"They let me in, and it wasn't long before I was in front of Jyn."

Radyn let out the breath he'd been holding. That, at least, was a different story than he'd expected.

"I told him what had happened, but he already knew about it. He told me that it was all a misunderstanding that would be cleared up soon. Went so far as to promise you'd be free before the end of the day. He told me to go to my workshop or return to the Gathering and enjoy my day."

A growl escaped in the back of Radyn's throat, and he realized he was still connected to his shards. He let his connection go. Jyn was something else. He'd known Radyn would take the deal, even then. "What did you do?"

"It didn't seem like there was much else to do. I trusted Jyn, at least in this, so I took his advice and returned to the workshop. I spent the whole afternoon working on some new creations now that I know what will trade well in Starfall."

Radyn couldn't help but smile. That was Aria, all right.

"About an hour ago, I decided to leave. I wanted to be

home when you returned. On my way home, someone snuck up behind me and hit me. They didn't give me any warning or anything."

It wasn't definitive proof, but it certainly lent credence to Aria's claim that her assailant had been clan. Ever since Whitehawk had fallen, she remained incredibly aware of her surroundings. She wasn't easy to sneak up on, and to attack her before she realized she was in danger required considerable speed.

He wanted to ask her questions, but she wasn't finished.

"After I was on the ground, he turned me over like I weighed nothing at all. He put both hands around my neck and choked me."

Radyn had been so distracted by the sight of her face he hadn't looked any further. His eyes traveled down, and he saw the faint bruising around her neck.

"I tried to fight, but I couldn't do a thing against him. It was like trying to punch my way through a steel wall. But while he was choking me, he leaned close and told me this was all your fault. That you were sticking your nose someplace it didn't belong. He told me to tell you that they can reach you anywhere and there's nothing you can do to stop them. So, if you don't want to lose me, you'll stop immediately."

Radyn's blood went cold. It was all he could do to remain in place and listen. "Did he leave you alone after that?" he asked.

The corner of her mouth turned up, though Radyn couldn't see what she found amusing in the situation. "He did."

Radyn trembled. Aria was the foundation of everything he'd become since Nightkeep's attack. He endured his public shame because he had her respect. A thousand mocking voices weighed less than her gentle approval.

He accepted that his gifts and his history were likely to lead him into danger, but he'd never thought his actions would cause someone to lash out at her so directly. Just imagining a day when he survived, and she didn't, brought his thoughts to a standstill.

"If they want me to stop, I'll stop. Now that I'm back home, there's nothing they can do."

"What did happen to you? Why were you arrested?"

Radyn related the whole story; from the moment the Shields had surrounded him at the Gathering to his return to Firestone. "I'd hoped that Jyn would give Nikki and I permission to return to Starfall and rattle their clan a bit. I'm not sure he'll want that, but it's the only way I had thought of to continue. There's nothing I can do here. But now that this has happened, I'll tell Nikki she's on her own. She's impressive, so she'll find a way forward without me."

Aria held out her hands and Radyn took them. He stood and lifted her to her feet. "I'd heal you, if you like."

He reached up to her face, but she gently stopped his hand with one of her own. She looked down at the ground between them but didn't speak.

"Aria?" he asked.

She pulled his hand down. "I don't want you to heal me."

"Why not? Doesn't it hurt?"

"It does, but I'll go to the healers later. It can't be you, because then the people watching you will know that you still have shards."

Radyn opened his mouth to argue but stopped. She was right. He could heal her, but then she'd be confined to the home to hide his abilities. If she went to a healer, they'd likely suspect Radyn had abused her, but she'd be able to wander freely without worrying about endangering his secret.

He hated that the healers would think so little of him, but what did it matter? It wasn't as though he'd been held in high esteem before.

He nodded. "Would you like me to come with, or would it be easier alone?"

It was a question he asked more than he cared to admit. Often, it was easier for her to run errands without him. His presence tended to lead to questions and looks that were bearable but frustrating. Trades became more expensive, and prices rose wherever he walked. Alone, she retained some measure of anonymity.

She shook her head. "I don't want you to come with me, but not because it'll be easier for me. You can't join me because I want you to keep working with Nikki."

"No." That decision, at least, came easy. "I won't be the reason you come to harm."

"I'm not sure you get to choose. We started dating when you were clan, and I always knew that our relationship would bear the burden of your calling. It's no different now."

"Except that it is. Now I'm a farmer caught up in something far beyond me. All I have to do to keep you safe is to step away. No harm will come to you if my only enemy is the elements and pernicious weeds."

"You don't believe that, not deep in your heart. I know you want to convince yourself that you're a farmer, that you've found some measure of the peace your father did, but that's not what I see. I see you sacrificing yourself day after day, and while farming might be something familiar, it's not what you seek."

Her words rang like a bell in his chest, dislodging a tightness he hadn't realized he possessed. As usual, she was right, though he didn't want to believe her.

"Even if that's true, it only means I need more time. It doesn't mean I need to rush to hold onto the remnants of a life that can no longer be mine."

She rubbed her thumb against the back of his hand, then turned his hand over and pressed it against the callouses on his palm. "I think that you need a new path, and this incident is showing you the way."

"Even if that much is true, it's not worth putting you at risk."

"And I'm honored you feel that way, even though you're acting like a fool. You can't protect me all the time and you'd be miserable if you tried. I've long accepted the dangers of being your partner, and that's still true today."

Her words choked his throat and he swallowed hard. She'd already endured too much in her life.

Her grin widened. "Besides, it's not as though I'm helpless. That Dagger that attacked already regrets his actions, of that, I'm sure."

He looked up. Even though the grin had to hurt with

the bruising on her cheek, she kept it in place. "What did you do?" he asked.

She held up a small, crushed canister. He'd seen it once before, but it took him a moment to recognize it. She'd shown it to him when she'd first been designing it. "You didn't. I didn't even realize you'd finished it."

"I did, and I'm pleased to report it works just as well as I hoped."

Despite everything, Radyn laughed out loud and shook his head. "Tell me about it."

"Once he started choking me, I was able to reach into my pocket and grab it. I closed my eyes, looked away, and broke it open. The powder didn't spread far, but the results were instant. He started screaming and grabbing at his face. I don't blame him. Despite my precautions, a bit of the powder got near my nose, and that was terrible enough."

Radyn had seen the harsh redness around Aria's nose but had assumed it had been from crying and blowing her nose too often.

"I followed him as he ran and stumbled away. At first, I was worried he might notice, but I think he was in too much pain for that. He made it to the surface and the last I saw of him, he was running toward the bridge that leads to Starfall."

Radyn kissed her hard, heart pounding as though he'd just finished a race. "You're a genius!"

"About time somebody noticed," she replied.

After his initial excitement died down, he looked her in her good eye. "Are you absolutely certain about this?"

She nodded without hesitation. "I'm grateful for your

concern, but I don't want to live with you sacrificing so much of yourself on my behalf. You belong on the hunt, and somewhere out there, there's a young woman who needs someone like you looking for her."

Radyn bowed deeply to her. "I love you, you know."

"I know. I love you, too."

Their moment was interrupted by a knock on the door. Radyn went to answer it, Aria just a few steps behind him. He opened the door and found Nikki waiting impatiently on the other side. "Honestly wasn't sure I was going to find you here," she admitted.

"No other place I'd rather be."

Nikki's gaze caught sight of Aria and her eyes widened. "What happened?"

"It seems our questions have been worrying some people, so they decided to threaten Aria."

"Radyn, I'm sorry, I had no idea—"

He cut her off. "You couldn't have. But it means we're on the right track. Did you get the permission from Jyn?"

"It was an argument, but yes. Starfall's Blade has been made aware, too, and although she isn't terribly happy about the idea, the Blade convinced her our investigation was in her best interests."

Good. They needed that hurdle cleared out of the way. "Then we have no time to waste. Thanks to Aria, the trail is fresh again."

Nikki looked to Aria for approval, and she nodded. She still debated for a moment, and that hesitation only solidified Radyn's impressions of her further. Nikki was a rare find, and he was glad Jyn had someone like her by his side.

"Fair enough," she finally said. "Let's go."

"Indeed," Radyn said, "because we've got some Daggers to hunt down, and we don't want to miss them."

Nikki swore under her breath at the mention of Daggers, but she didn't try to stop him as he kissed Aria farewell and charged out the door, eager to find the fool who had threatened everything he held dear.

12

———————

Nikki followed Radyn up the stairs toward the surface. She'd been quiet since they'd left Radyn's house, but he couldn't guess the nature of the thoughts that consumed her. It wasn't until they were only two levels beneath the surface that she spoke. "Aria is an impressive woman."

"You don't need to tell me," Radyn said. "I learn that truth anew every day."

"I did some research on her before I ran over to recruit you from your cell. I thought it might be useful if you proved unreasonable. She's a survivor of the fall of Whitehawk, right?"

"Pulled her out of the ruins with the help of my roommates. I was an initiate at the time."

"Does she know what really happened the day Nightkeep attacked?"

Radyn stopped in his tracks and turned to stare at her. "You really don't give up, do you?"

"I wouldn't be a very good Shield if I did."

Radyn bit back his retort. Most Shields were nothing like Nikki, but Firestone would be an even better city to live in if they were.

He almost said that yes, she did, but that would be the same as admitting there was a deeper truth to the day of the raid. Nikki already clearly suspected, but he wasn't going to be the one who confirmed it for her. He'd given Jyn his word. Instead, he turned back and hurried up the stairs.

His brief connection with the shards had wiped the exhaustion from his body. The strength wouldn't last as long as that which came from a full night of sleep, but it would keep him moving for a while yet.

He turned the discussion away. "Were you able to learn anything more about Josiah?"

"Not as much as I wanted. I spoke to his master, but the man didn't have much useful to say. I got the sense they didn't spend all that much time together."

"That's not unusual. What did he say?"

"That Josiah had all the makings of a great Dagger, but no more. He was a diligent enough student and mastered the basic techniques easily enough, and it sounded like he had the ambition to be a great Sword. He didn't take to the shards too well, though. His master implied Josiah had barely passed the tests for Dagger and didn't think he'd ever make it to Sword."

Radyn grimaced. The same description could apply to dozens of the initiates he'd trained with. "Surely there had to be something more interesting about him."

"I asked the same question. The only answer the master could give me was that Josiah was more interested in shard lore than most. His obsession deepened as it became clear that he lacked the affinity to become a Sword."

They paused their conversation as they reached the Shields standing guard on the Firestone side of the bridge. Nikki got them through quickly.

"That's still not much. But if this whole mess has something to do with Engines or shards, it might explain why he was involved. An obsession with the Engine can lead to some interesting places," Radyn said.

"You sound as though you speak from experience."

Radyn nodded. "A story for another day, perhaps."

"It's starting to sound like you're full of them."

Radyn ignored the jibe as Nikki's papers admitted them onto Starfall. He paused to bother one of the guards before he moved on to the next visitor in line. "Excuse me, but if I get hurt, where's the closest place to find a healer?"

The Shield looked exasperated, more from what had certainly been a long day of answering questions than Radyn in particular. But he forced a tired smile to his face and pointed toward the center of the surface. "There's a cluster of healing tents that way. You should be able to get whatever help you need there, but try not to go unless it's really needed. Our healers have been busy all day."

"Of course, thank you very much." Radyn bowed deeply. The guard turned to the next visitor in line and promptly forgot about him.

"You don't think he would have gone straight to the healers at the academy?" Nikki asked.

"It's possible, but I doubt it. There would be a lot of

questions, and I'm guessing he wasn't in Firestone on official clan duties. Here on the surface, he'd at least be able to escape the worst of the questioning. If the healers are as busy as that Shield said, they might not even care to ask anything."

Nikki accepted the explanation and followed him. If nothing else, if he was wrong, Jyn's letter would give them access to Starfall's academy. But if the Dagger had gone there, it implied an official approval Radyn didn't want to consider.

Healing tents first. He could worry about the consequences later.

They found the site without too much difficulty, thanks in large part to the line outside its entrance. Most of the injuries appeared linked to excessive ale consumption. Radyn and Nikki ignored the line and walked to the entrance, where they were stopped by a young healer's apprentice. "Back of the line like everyone else."

Nikki flashed her papers at the young man. "We're not here for healing. We're looking for someone who might be here."

The apprentice looked up, his eyes bloodshot, and he finally noticed Nikki's uniform. He bowed hastily. "Oh, sorry, ma'am. I didn't know. It's been a long day."

"It's no problem." Nikki gestured for Radyn to continue.

Radyn picked up where Nikki had dropped off. "We're looking for a young man. He would be suffering from severely irritated eyes and nostrils, at the very least."

"Ahh, yes. He's here. Name's Ty, and he's in that tent

resting. My master complained it was one of the more difficult healings he's attempted lately."

Radyn suppressed the grin that threatened to bloom on his face. Aria had been hurt, but she'd given even worse than she'd received, if Radyn had to guess. He bowed. "Thank you."

The apprentice nodded absent-mindedly, then turned his attention to the next poor soul in line.

"Can you stand watch at the entrance?" Radyn asked Nikki.

She looked immediately suspicious. "If you think I'm going to let you speak to a suspect who hurt your wife alone, you're mad."

"I won't kill him."

She snorted. "There's a wide stretch between that promise and the limit of what I'd consider acceptable."

"You know clan members won't speak to Shields. I think he'd be more—shall we say, persuadable—if you let me speak to him alone. You can stand at the entrance and babysit. But someone should keep an eye out for trouble."

"The greatest trouble we're going to have is you," she said, but her retort lacked her earlier conviction. She couldn't argue his point about clan members not showing Shields the respect they typically deserved.

On paper, Shields occupied a place of honor beside the clan, but in reality, it was anything but. Most Shields were failed clan initiates, so the clan members enjoyed an inherent sense of superiority to start. Beyond that, though, it was the clan that was esteemed above all else. They had the strength and the honor, and there was little the Shields could do if clan members didn't cooperate. In truth, Daggers and Swords were only punished by the clan when they wandered too far from established traditions.

Nikki gritted her teeth and said, "Fine. But watch yourself, because I'll be watching you. I don't need another corpse on my hands today."

Radyn nodded and entered the tent. Nikki came in, too, but pulled one of the flaps aside so she could look out into the night.

Radyn's grin stretched from ear to ear when he caught his first sight of the injured Dagger. Aria's creation had been every bit as effective as she'd planned. It didn't kill, but the Dagger's eyes were still puffy and swollen. Tears leaked uncontrollably down the side of his face and his entire nose was inflamed and red.

And this was after the healer had worked with him.

"Who are you?" the Dagger asked.

Radyn guessed Ty's sight was still blurry, so he stepped close. "Aria told me you had a message for me, so I came to hear it personally."

Ty breathed in sharply, but Radyn had been ready. He smashed his fist into Ty's stomach, driving the air from his lungs and choking off his shout before it left his lips.

Ty coughed and spit as he gasped for air. Radyn ignored his struggles as he drew a small steel knife from his pocket. He reached down. Like most Daggers, Ty wore a wide leather band around his wrist. The band served both as protection and as the keeper of a clan member's shards. The shard pressed against the skin, and Radyn didn't want Ty to have that strength available to him. He gripped the wrist tight, immobilizing it for the moment he required to slide the knife through the cord that held the band closed and cut it away.

Radyn ripped the band off Ty's wrist and placed it on his own.

Ty's free left hand scrambled for the hilt at his belt. Radyn connected with the new shard and shot his arm out, grabbing the hand and the weapon as Ty pulled it free. Radyn twisted hard and tore it out of Ty's grip. Then he swung his fist at Ty's face.

He kept his strength in check, but Ty's face still snapped to the side and his eyes went glassy. Radyn positioned himself better in the moment of confusion, and once Ty's gaze focused again, he pressed the opening of the hilt against the side of Ty's head. "It's been a long time since I've gotten to hold one of these. Can't do it on Firestone, because the clan will kill me. Here, though, I think I'll get away with it. Give me one good reason why I shouldn't connect to the shards in the hilt."

Ty's eyes were as wide as saucers, and he blubbered incoherently. He looked a few years younger than Radyn, but his gaze was soft. Beating up Aria was probably the most violent thing he'd ever done in his service.

After trying and failing to get the hilt away from his skull, his whimpering settled into language Radyn could understand. "It wasn't my idea!"

That didn't surprise Radyn. From what little he'd seen of Ty, the Dagger would probably need help to fight his way out of an ill-fitting robe. He needed information he could act on. "So, who told you to threaten her?"

Ty gulped and shook his head.

Radyn raised the fist with sword in hand, but when Ty still didn't speak, he didn't deliver the blow. Ty expected it. He was preparing for it. Soon, it wouldn't scare him like it had. No, he needed something new.

He brought the hilt back to the side of Ty's face, but instead of pressing the opening against his skull, he twisted it to the side so the hilt was parallel to Ty's cheek. Then he connected with the shards within.

He couldn't lie. It had been months since he'd connected with a maniblade, and he'd missed the feeling of having one in hand. The blades didn't sing like the Engine did, but they were a part of the music all the same. Using one brought him closer to the bliss the Engine promised.

"Radyn! What are you doing?" Nikki whisper-shouted.

"Reminding our Dagger that actions have consequences. But don't worry, I'll try to make sure none of the wounds are fatal."

"This is why I didn't want you to be a part of this!" Nikki was torn between staring out the tent and watching Radyn to ensure he didn't go too far. Though from the look in her eyes, part of her believed he already had.

Radyn turned all his attention back to Ty. "You can probably fight with one eye, can't you?"

He brought the maniblade closer to Ty's left eye. All of Ty's struggles ceased as the blade came within an inch of his face. He looked desperately in Nikki's direction. "Ma'am, he's mad!"

Radyn twisted the maniblade so he could press the

flat of the weapon against Ty's eyebrow. The Dagger whimpered and closed his eyes.

"I don't think even she wants to save you. She saw Aria's face and knows what kind of monster you are. She'd probably be fine if I took an eye."

"It was for the city!" Ty cried.

Radyn's blood turned to ice in his veins. "The Blade ordered this?"

"No, no, not that. I'm sorry, but I can't tell you. They kill anyone who spills their secrets."

"And I'll kill you if you don't. Seems like you've got a real problem you need to figure out. If it helps you decide, I'm here right now, and they're not."

Ty quivered under Radyn's grip but didn't answer. Radyn pressed the side of the maniblade harder against Ty's face. Ty winced but still didn't confess.

He witnessed the moment Ty reached his decision. His quivering and whimpering ceased. His eyes continued to water, but that was due more to Aria than anyone else. When he spoke again, his voice trembled only a little. "Do what you must. I fight for humanity."

Radyn's heart sank. It was possible he could still break Ty, but the cost was higher than he was willing to pay.

He'd failed.

"Radyn, I think we've got a problem," Nikki said.

"What?"

"Someone's coming. They're debating whether or not to stay in line right now, but they've got a maniblade at their hip."

"A Sword?"

"Don't know. He's not wearing a uniform, but he's got a full view of the healing tents." Nikki withdrew her head back into the tent, leaving only the slimmest crack for her to look out of.

Before the Dagger could ruin their evening more, Radyn punched him in the face using more of his shard-assisted strength. Ty's eyes rolled up in his head as he lost consciousness. Radyn was tempted to spit on him, but they didn't have the time if a clan member was close.

"Come on," he said as he gestured to Nikki. "We can sneak out the back."

There was no flap on the back of the tent, but the healing center was only temporary. The canvas had been loosely staked down, making it easy for them to slide under. Nikki was about to walk away, but Radyn waited.

"What are you doing?" she whispered.

"Waiting. Perhaps they'll talk."

She looked at him like he was mad, which was becoming quite a common occurrence.

Nikki swore but didn't run. They crouched together on the outside of the tent, earning odd looks from passersby going to and from their own events at the Gathering. Fortunately, there was no shortage of unusual behavior thanks to the event, so no one bothered them.

They hadn't left a moment too soon. A minute after they'd settled, Radyn heard the front of the tent flap open. Slow, confident footsteps entered and stopped by the bed. Radyn breathed slowly as the silence in the tent stretched out.

The visitor cursed softly but didn't move. Radyn

connected with his shards so that he could listen better, but all he heard was the man's breathing.

He appreciated that Nikki had been sharp enough to spot the visitor in time. Not many would have seen the hilt and known who was coming. She'd given them another possible lead.

He heard sudden movement inside the tent, followed by the sounds of surprise and struggle. Someone gagged and gasped for air. Nikki heard the sounds, too, and twisted as though she was going to cut her way through the tent to stop the assault. Radyn laid a cautioning hand on her arm and shook his head.

She glared at him, but it was over before they could argue. The struggles ceased. Thanks to his sharper senses, Radyn could listen to the rhythm of the assailant's breath. It hadn't changed a bit.

Bitter bile rose in his throat. Becoming a killer was part of the price of joining the clan. Cities needed warriors for protection, and that burden fell squarely upon the select few who passed the trials of their clan. Radyn had taken lives while doing his duty, and though the memories still haunted him at night, he took some small measure of comfort in knowing his sacrifices had protected his city.

Robyn's murder, and now this one, wasn't necessary. They were senseless, but they didn't disturb the killer in the tent enough to affect his breathing.

The Sword stepped outside the tent. He called out, concern and panic in his voice. "Apprentice, did you see his two visitors leave?"

"No, sir, but it's been busy, so I might have missed them."

"Call the Shields! I think my friend has been murdered."

Nikki swore and looked around. She leaned in close to Radyn. "I'm thinking that maybe it's time to go."

Radyn agreed. He had no interest in being arrested for the second time in one day. As they snuck away from the tent, he wondered if, by the end of the night, he'd be wanted by every Shield and clan member in both cities.

The way his day was going, it was looking increasingly likely.

13

R adyn and Nikki had just escaped into the crowd when he came to a stop. She noticed a moment later and stopped, too, half-turning to see what the problem was. He stared hard at the ground, fists clenched.

After another moment with no answer, she asked, "What's wrong?"

He licked his lips. "I'm tired of running, and it's getting us nowhere." He thrust out his thumb in the direction of the healing tents. "That man knows what's happening. I say we ask him."

"He's Starfall's clan, and you're not even Firestone's. You might have stolen Ty's shards and hilt, but you haven't been active for almost a year. Jyn's papers won't protect you from the trouble you're about to stir up."

"I didn't need Jyn's protection when I was a Sword, and I don't need it now. I'm not going to run the other way when I see evil men in front of me."

"You can't fight against these people! We need

evidence and proof, then we bring the full might of Firestone and Starfall down on them."

"You're assuming that even if we found such proof, we'd find aid. I trust Jyn well enough, but have you ever wondered how high up this goes in Starfall? They have all the shardbearers in this city looking for the missing girl. You can't do that if you're just a lowly Dagger."

Nikki worked her jaw back and forth as though she'd just been punched. "It's still a damn foolish thing to do."

"You'll find no argument here. I'll understand if you don't want to help. The smartest thing to do is probably return to Jyn and tell him everything that's happened."

She finally turned fully toward him. "I don't think he'd be too pleased if I returned without you, especially to tell him I let you go ahead on your own."

"You'll help, then?"

She nodded.

"Good. I think we need to split apart and keep close to the crowds. They'll be looking for the two of us together, but they might not notice us if we're apart. Do you have something to cover your hair? It's rather distinct."

"I'm sure I can find something," she said.

"Good. We wait for the killer to leave the healing grounds, then we'll follow him until he gets someplace quiet. Then we'll ask him our questions."

Nikki gave a little snort. "And if he's not too willing to answer our questions? Or if he wants to fight?"

"No point worrying about that until it happens. For now, let's just get him alone."

"Fair enough." She made to leave, then stopped. "But you never saw him. How are you going to know—"

"I'll know," he said.

Her doubt only lasted for a moment and then she nodded. "Good luck."

"You, too."

They parted ways and Radyn charted a course through the moving crowds, blending with group after group as they passed by the healing tents. He found a dark shadow behind a merchant's tent and pressed himself into it. Then he waited.

The shardbearer's announcement had caused quite a stir in the healing grounds. Shields arrived and spoke with a tall man with long blond hair. The man spoke with a sense of easy authority, and the Shields listened closely.

Radyn focused on the tall man. He looked to be somewhere in his late thirties, and tonight, he was dressed in a tight-fitting black tunic and pants. The clothes clung to his body as though they were afraid they might fall off. The man's biceps bulged even at rest. He looked like the sort of shardbearer the clan would send to the schools to convince students to attempt the trials.

Despite his striking appearance, or maybe even because of it, Radyn felt a sense of discomfort pass over him as he watched the man calmly instruct the Shields on how to investigate the murder he'd committed. Had Radyn not known the man had killed Ty, he'd never have suspected him.

That ability, not just to lie but to act so convincingly, sent a chill down his spine. He thought he'd confronted evil before, but now he wasn't so sure. Nuela's plan to abandon Firestone to the surface somehow seemed less upsetting than the phony, heartfelt sorrow on the shardbearer's face.

The process of directing the Shields took time. Radyn used it to watch and observe. Hopefully Nikki would find some way to cover her hair. The murderer spoke to the Shields, sincerity oozing from his pores. The healer's apprentice gave them a description, and then the shardbearer took his leave. He left the healer's tents and looked around before walking away.

Radyn waited a few moments, following the murderer with his eyes before leaving the safety of the shadows. He walked close to groups, always keeping them between him and the Starfall shardbearer. The murderer stopped several times at merchant stands, but he never bought anything. He used the opportunities to glance around, but Radyn never felt as though he was in danger of being noticed.

The man played at being aware of his surroundings, just as he pretended to be honorable.

Radyn tamped down the excitement that threatened to distract him. The murderer didn't have many reasons to be so paranoid. Radyn could well imagine checking once or twice to ensure the Shields weren't interested in him, but after the fifth stop, Radyn decided the murderer had another appointment tonight. One he didn't want others following him to.

The shardbearer looked around one last time before entering a grove. Lamps had been hung on tree branches, illuminating paths for couples to walk. The man hurried down one of the paths, brushing rudely past a pair of couples who shot him annoyed looks.

Radyn watched from outside the grove, then looked around before entering. Lines of sight would be shorter within, and he didn't want to walk into a trap. Nothing he saw alarmed him. The Gathering proceeded apace, no one wise to the murder and violence that tainted the festivities. Nikki was well behind him, watching to see what he would do. She'd wrapped a scarf around her head as though to ward off the chill of the night.

He gave her a quick nod, then ducked into the grove. He followed the lit paths until there was a gap in the trees, then slipped into the shadows. A pair of lovers were pressed up against a tree, too distracted by each other's bodies to notice as he slipped silently within a few paces of them. He stepped carefully, avoiding twigs and leaves that would snap and give away his position. He paralleled the path until he saw a small clearing.

A bench sat in the middle of the clearing. It was bathed in light, making approaching it without being seen impossible. Two men sat together, and at least one of them had murdered a Dagger in the last hour. The other one was older, his white hair tied into a tight tail at the back of his neck. They sat close and leaned in, speaking softly. Their conversation paused anytime someone came close, but they seemed plenty patient.

Radyn frowned. Why meet in a place like this? He supposed it was private enough but was too much trouble. All they had to do was go to the other's homes and no one could listen in.

For the moment, he didn't question his good fortune. He tucked himself deep into the shadows and became perfectly still. He connected with all his shards, from the ones in his body to the ones he'd just stolen. Eventually, he'd have to get rid of those. If the Shields were looking for any evidence of his guilt, the shards would be more than enough.

That was a problem for another time, though. Same with the hilt. It could come in very useful soon.

For now, he focused his sharpened senses on the bench.

"You didn't have to kill him," the old man said.

"It was only a matter of time. These young ones, they're so eager to believe in something that their faith is groundless and easily challenged. If he didn't talk, he would have soon."

The old man grunted but didn't argue the point. "It's messy, is all."

"I thought it was quite elegant, actually. I took care of one problem before it became serious and handed another one to Radyn and his annoying friend. It'll make it that much harder for them now."

"I'm still not convinced it was necessary, but we can argue the point later. We believe we are getting close to finding the girl."

The murderer nodded. "About time. I thought you would have found her by now."

"I'm not sure if the Singers I assigned to the task aren't sensitive enough or if there is something more at play. It's possible she's found a way to disguise herself, but there aren't many places in the city we haven't looked."

"And you're sure she's the one?"

The older man spread his hands and shrugged. "I don't know if she's the one we've been waiting for, but she's the best candidate we've found. She traveled through the Engines. There's no other way she could be on board. We've interrogated every guard who worked within three days of her appearance. No one slacked in their duty."

"Maybe they'd reconsider if I spoke with them."

"There is a time and a place for your methods, Markus, but not every problem is solved with a maniblade."

The murderer scoffed. "I've yet to find one."

"Regardless, we're close. I can send a messenger to the academy when it's time. You've selected your warriors."

"All my best." From Radyn's vantage point, Markus looked eager to call them now.

"Good. We should have the girl and her allies trapped by the end of the night. My Singers tell me it will be early morning at the latest."

Markus stood. "Then let's hope they're right. I'll be waiting for your message."

He strode away from the bench, leaving the older man alone in the clearing. The man, who Radyn assumed was a Singer, leaned back and stared at the sky through the opening in the trees.

Radyn disconnected from his shards. He briefly considered speaking with the Singer but saw little point. He'd learned enough, and for the moment, they didn't know how much he knew. With some luck, he could turn that to his advantage.

He waited in the shadows a bit longer, but the Singer seemed in no hurry to depart. Radyn crept away, ensuring once again that no noises betrayed his presence. Once he was out of sight, he returned to the lit path and exited the grove. He nodded in Nikki's direction and started back toward the bridge. She hurried to catch up.

"What did you learn?"

"Enough. At least, I think I have an idea of what's happening. We need to get to Jyn and let him know. This goes deeper than any either of us are capable of handling on our own."

"About time you saw reason."

As they neared the bridge, Radyn pulled Nikki aside. He cursed his own foolishness. The cities were similar enough that he sometimes forgot what it meant that he was here and not on Firestone. Beside him, Nikki cursed, too.

The Starfall end of the bridge was swarming with Shields, and they were checking everyone leaving with a thoroughness that made their intent clear. Radyn begrudgingly gave Markus credit. He hadn't seen many Shields since leaving the grove, but now he knew why. They'd all been tasked with the duy of keeping him here. He could fight his way through them, but that wouldn't end well for anyone.

"Any great ideas?" he asked.

Nikki thought for a moment, then shook her head. "It'll take hours, at least, to get through to Jyn. And that's if they treat us well and uphold their end of the city agreements. With a Dagger dead, that's far from guaranteed."

The bridge was the only path off the city, but was there another way?

Radyn chuckled to himself. "Are you interested in a truly horrible idea?"

Nikki's eyebrow looked like it was about to jump off her forehead it arched so high. "Considering how poor your average idea is, I'm not sure I want to know."

"Come with me." He turned and left the bridge behind, walking into the dark and away from the lights and music of this evening's Gathering. It didn't take long for them to reach the edge of the city. A waist-high fence of wooden posts and double crossbeams marked the safe edge.

"Radyn? What are you thinking?" Nikki held back, walking at least five paces away from him.

All children were taught to avoid the edges of cities. Farmland typically stopped at least ten to fifteen feet from the edge, and the fence was built four or five feet in, so even if someone was foolish enough to climb over, there was some degree of safety on the other side.

Typically, every handful of years, there would be a story of a group of children daring each other to jump over the fence. Inevitably, a strong gust of wind or an unfortunate trip would send one of the children plummeting to the surface below, and the children would avoid it for a few years.

A few adults took the jump, too, most willingly. It was a selfish way to die, taking the body's resources away from the city without consideration, but Radyn had always understood. Now that he'd experienced flight for himself, he thought that a long fall and a sudden end wasn't a bad way to travel to the gate.

He had no such plans today.

"Radyn?" Nikki repeated, clearly fearing that he had lost his mind.

And perhaps he had. As far as he knew, no one even spoke of such feats in legends. "I think we should jump."

Nikki shook her head. "No."

She took a few steps away, still shaking her head. "No. No. I think I'll take my chances with the bridge."

He held out his hand. "I'll need you if we're going to get to Jyn. Otherwise, the clan is just going to kill me."

"You can't jump! What are you thinking?"

"I'll call Tanwen," he said.

"Tanwen?"

"My dragon."

"You don't have a dragon anymore. You're not clan. Why can't you understand that?" She drew her scarf back and pulled at her hair.

"Normally, you'd be right, but I saved Tanwen's life during Nightkeep's raid. It turns out he doesn't like having any other riders anymore, so he's still mine. He stays at the nest and Macken keeps trying to breed him. The sense I get from Tanwen is that he's living a pretty good life. He gets most of the rewards of partnering with humans with little of the work. I'm sure he wouldn't mind lending me a hand today."

Nikki shook her head again. "You're mad. Stark. Raving. Mad. How are you even still alive?"

Radyn ignored her question. "Are you coming? If I land at the nest without you, I'll end up in even more trouble than I am right now. It'll be easy. I'll just ask Tanwen to fly close and slow. We take a running leap, jump, and he'll carry us right home, with no one the wiser."

This time, she came closer to the fence before shaking her head and retreating. Radyn made no sudden moves. He feared that if he did, she'd bolt like a deer discovering a hunter nearby.

There was only one other card to play. "If you come with me, I'll ask Jyn for permission to tell you the truth about what happened to me. I can't promise he'll agree, but I'll ask."

Her uncertainty transformed into a glare. "That's just cruel."

"We'll be fine. And if we aren't, at least you'll have the pleasure of saying 'I told you so' right before we both die."

"Fine."

Radyn climbed over the fence, then held out his hand to help her. She ignored the hand and climbed over herself, but she kept both hands on the nearest crossbeam.

Radyn closed his eyes, connected with his shards, and sought out Tanwen. His awareness stretched through the Song of the Engine and around a bright presence he'd not ever sensed before. He ignored it to seek Tanwen's comforting familiarity.

The dragon greeted him warmly and Radyn asked for his help. As he'd hoped, a deep sense of satisfaction answered his request.

He opened his eyes and chuckled as he imagined the chaos Tanwen was surely causing at the nest. Macken would be stomping around and swearing up a storm, but it wasn't long before Tanwen was in the air. That was one nice part of having a dragon as an ally. Few people ever told a dragon no.

"He's coming," he told Nikki. He held out his hand and this time she took it. Her fingers were cold and clammy.

Tanwen circled up high once, and through a second sight, Radyn looked down at the five cities. Firestone was in the center of the formation, and at the moment, it looked as though it was surrounded by enemies.

Tanwen banked down, then bled speed. Radyn could sense his friend approaching through their bond, but he couldn't see anything in the darkness of night.

"It'll only be a moment or two, now. When I tell you to run, you'll need to run as fast as you can. Jump as far as you can, too."

Before she had time to argue, Tanwen arrived.

"Now!"

Radyn pulled her behind him, but after a step she, too, ran as fast as she could. They covered the last distance in two more steps, and they leaped.

They missed Tanwen, but Radyn had never expected to jump onto a moving dragon. They fell and Tanwen chased after them. It caught them gently on its broad back and slowly pulled up. Radyn found a grip under one of Tanwen's scales and locked both him and Nikki in place.

Once she was securely positioned she swore at him and slapped him, but fresh strength flooded through his limbs. He laughed out loud as the cities fell behind them.

For a moment, he'd succeeded in leaving all his problems behind.

"I told you it would work," he said, sounding more confident than he'd been just moments ago.

She swore again but then relaxed. He gave her a moment to work through the fear and excitement she was no doubt feeling. Once he was certain she had a hold, he clambered forward and onto Tanwen's neck. He embraced the dragon. "It's good to see you again, friend."

Tanwen roared with delight as they fled through the night. Eventually, Radyn turned Tanwen toward Firestone.

They didn't have much time to waste, but he'd have to risk his life before he could save the girl's. It was time to see an old ally.

14

————

Radyn reveled in the brief moments of flight. One consequence of having his name bloodied was losing his access to the nest, and of everything he endured, that was perhaps what he regretted the most. Tanwen got along fine without him, but he sensed the dragon's satisfaction at their reunion. Dragons were meant to fly.

He leaned against Tanwen's neck. "Once this is over, I'll be able to fly with you again."

Tanwen rumbled with pleasure.

Radyn turned back to Nikki. "Hold on tight. It should be a gentle landing, but I'd hate to have you get hurt now after all we've been through."

She clutched the dragon's scales until her knuckles turned white. Her eyes were as wide as coins. It was the first time he'd seen her frightened.

He'd been the same way on his first flight. He'd come close to messing his pants that day. It was a good thing he hadn't. He wouldn't have made nearly the same impression on Aria as he had.

Tanwen landed in the middle of the nest's staging area, and it didn't take long for Macken to come charging over. When he saw Radyn on top of Tanwen, he turned as red as a ripe tomato. "What in the name of the gate do you think you're doing!" he yelled.

Radyn dismounted Tanwen and dropped lightly to the ground. "Figured it was time to take Tanwen for a ride. He and I haven't been in the air for a while."

He took a step away from Macken, but a maniblade sprang to life and blocked his exit. Macken growled.

"You know damn well what this means, Radyn. You've always been good to Tanwen, but Jyn's orders were clear."

Radyn was grateful Macken hadn't tried to cut him down already. The Sword liked to bluster and certainly did his part to frighten initiates, but at heart, he was a kind man. He didn't want to cut Radyn down any more than Radyn wanted to be cut down. Radyn had saved Tanwen's life during Nightkeep's attack. In so doing, he'd made two allies for life.

Nikki interrupted Macken before the situation could devolve further. She finished clambering down from Tanwen and hurried to stand between the two shardbearers. She thrust Jyn's orders in front of Macken's face, brandishing them like a maniblade.

Macken grabbed the papers with his free hand and studied them. He never let his maniblade drop, though. Then he handed the papers back to Nikki. "This doesn't concern the Shields."

"Radyn has been helping me investigate a series of

crimes committed on Starfall. During our investigation, the bridge was closed to us by Starfall's authorities. Radyn felt he had little choice but to call Tanwen. He and the dragon might very well have saved our lives tonight."

Macken's gaze traveled between the two of them. "Can't say it's too hard to believe you've been causing trouble again. Doesn't mean you can bend the rules this far, though."

Nikki looked around the nest. At this time of night, it was quiet. The three of them were the only ones in the landing zone. "We need to speak with the Blade as quickly as possible. Can you arrange that? We'll want someplace quiet where no one will see us or the Blade meeting."

Macken's eyes narrowed, and he cast the full force of his gaze on Radyn.

The former Sword nodded. "Something has come up. I'd appreciate it if you could summon Jyn. If he wants to kill me after for what I did, I won't even argue."

Macken snorted, but he let the maniblade vanish. "You're a pain in my ass, but sometimes I can't help but think the clan needs more like you. You certainly keep life interesting." He pointed his hilt at one of the dark buildings behind him. "No one will be in there until morning. You two can wait in there. I'll send a messenger for the Blade."

Radyn bowed. "Thank you."

Macken grunted. "You're just lucky Tanwen still likes you. I wouldn't want to cut you down and break his heart."

Macken was as good as his word. Jyn arrived within the hour. He checked all the windows to ensure the blinds were closed and no one could see in, then sat down heavily. Radyn had arranged a small, rickety table so that he and Nikki sat on one side and Jyn on the other.

Jyn and Radyn studied one another, and Radyn wondered what Jyn noticed about him.

Almost a year had passed since they'd seen each other last, and Radyn had halfway expected they'd never be in the same room again. Responsibility had changed Jyn. He'd always been strong, always been clever, but his emotions ran deep now. Radyn stared into his face and didn't have the slightest clue what he was thinking. He'd put on more muscle since they'd last crossed paths, too. An impressive feat considering the demands on his time.

"Did you come alone?" Radyn asked.

"Magni is outside, but he doesn't know who's in here. He's furious about it."

Radyn nodded. "He's a good man. You're fortunate to have him by your side."

Jyn's weight shifted forward. The old chair groaned. "I didn't come here to listen to you tell me things I already know. I'd be well within my rights to cut you down right now for summoning Tanwen."

Radyn didn't flinch at Jyn's threat. "It's about the Engine."

Jyn's expressions were subtle, but Radyn didn't miss the sudden concern that passed over his face. He leaned back and swore. "Tell me."

"Everything revolves around a girl. I don't know who she is, but I think there are two factions fighting over her. Josiah was part of one. Whatever that group wants, they were willing to torture an old cook for information on the girl. The second group has the girl now, and I'd guess it was one of them that killed Josiah. I know nothing about them except that they're being hunted by the first group."

Nikki shot him an angry glare and he silently asked for her forgiveness. He'd only figured that much out after listening to Markus and the Singer. Since then, he hadn't had time to explain it to her.

Jyn pressed his thumb and forefinger against the bridge of his nose. "Why is this girl so important?"

"I believe she is gifted in some way. I overheard a conversation between two members of the group Josiah belonged to. One was a Starfall Sword and the other a Singer. They implied the girl had the ability to travel from one Engine to another."

Jyn dropped his hand and looked up. "That's impossible."

"Before tonight, I would have agreed with you. It still seems impossible. But people are killing one another over what they believe she's can do."

Jyn stared at the ceiling. "Tell me everything."

Radyn did, speaking quickly. Nikki contributed what she had learned from investigating Josiah and confirmed Radyn's deductions. When they finished, Jyn stood up and paced the small room.

"None of this could have come at a worse time," he said.

"How are the talks going?" Radyn asked.

"Better than I expected. But now I need to ask myself if the other Blades are aware of what's happening in their cities. I have a hard time believing Tasha knows, but I can't speak for Arik. He keeps his secrets close."

Jyn wanted to say more, but he kept casting quick glances at Nikki. She picked up on his hesitation and called it out. "I'll leave if you want, but it sounds as if you think what's happening in the talks may affect the investigation. So, if I leave, I won't be as effective as I might have been. And after all I've done for you, I feel like I deserve more of your trust."

Jyn didn't debate for long. He sat back down and leaned forward, inviting them to do the same, as though they were conspirators in a deadly game. "The true purpose of this Gathering isn't to establish a new peace agreement between Firestone and Nightkeep. It's to address the question of the Engines."

Nikki's sharp mind leaped ahead. "They're failing, aren't they?"

"Our Singers believe so. They argue that the cities were never designed to stay aloft for as long as they have. It's frustrating how little we know for sure, but all three Blades gathered here believe we need to prepare for a new age. Last year, Nightkeep attempted to establish one by force. Now they're trying less costly forms of persuasion."

"What are they proposing?" Radyn asked.

"They've advanced a variety of proposals," Jyn said. "Some of more merit than others, but I believe they hope to absorb Firestone and Starfall into Nightkeep. It's the question I've been wrestling with since before the bridges were built."

Radyn was on his feet, pressing his hands down so hard against the table he felt the legs bend. "You'd consider that after what they did to us? Elora died to save us from them."

Jyn cast him a look of annoyance. "If it means the survival of this city and the protection of the people within, yes, I'll absolutely consider it. My duty is deeper than your desire for vengeance."

Jyn's certainty was like a bucket of cold water thrown on Radyn's face. "But why?"

"There's little doubt we're stronger together. Our antagonism is more a product of history than reality. Once, the cities had to fight one another for the meager resources of the surface, but now we know how to maintain stable populations. There are now more resources on the surface than there are people in the air to use them. I'm sure you haven't been to Nightkeep since the Gathering began, but their people are well-fed and want for nothing. If prosperity for my people means I need to kill my pride as a Blade, I consider that a small price to pay."

Radyn felt very much the child in the face of Jyn's dedication to his duty. He slumped back down in his chair. He'd always respected Jyn but had forgotten why he made such a good Blade.

When Jyn continued, his voice had lost some of its fire. "Staying together would also mean more support if the worst was to happen. Imagine how many people died on Whitehawk because no one was nearby. If our Singers noticed something wrong with the Engine, we could move people and supplies to another city before we fell. If we fell suddenly, the other cities would be there to rescue the survivors immediately."

Radyn thought of Jelrik and the other Singers hurrying in secret to Nightkeep. "At least some of the Singers are already cooperating with the other cities, aren't they?"

Jyn nodded. "Even if we don't reach a formal agreement, there's no harm in exchanging Singers. Perhaps one of them will figure out how to get us out of this mess."

The objection loomed large in Radyn's thoughts. "All of that assumes we can trust Nightkeep. They've not dealt honestly with us in the past."

Jyn nodded. "Agreed. Tasha speaks constantly of the benefits. She speaks of a world in which we share Singers and resources. Even our clans could train together and eventually become one. But I fear that if Firestone becomes a vassal to Nightkeep, we'll be treated as a different class of citizen. That our best and brightest will move to their cities and leave us the dregs."

He ran his hand across his bald scalp. "But I can't deny the potential of an alliance. The true challenge is reaching an agreement that is mutually beneficial."

"Which is why you're worried about the girl," Radyn said.

"If what you say is true, and she can travel between Engines, what else might she be able to do? Could she sing to an Engine alone? Command the fate of a city by herself? Could she cause an Engine to fail? It would help tremendously, too, if we knew more about the people seeking to capture her. What do they want?"

Jyn sighed and ran a hand through his hair. "The only way to know, and the only way to ensure she doesn't disrupt our negotiations, is to have her here, under our control."

"She's a young woman, not a tool to control," Radyn argued. Nikki's eyes went a little wider at the casual disrespect in his tone.

Jyn's gaze went flat. "I'm not saying that I approve, but it is the way of the world. If she can't be controlled, the only way we remain safe is if we kill her. Those are the only two choices, for Firestone's sake."

"For all we know, she might be the key to unlocking the mysteries of the Engines!" Radyn protested. "Would you destroy that because you're afraid?"

"Absolutely," Jyn said, stopping Radyn's tirade before it went too far. "Once again, you forget that my concerns are different than yours. Let us say there is only a small chance that this girl poses an incredible threat to us. Do you risk the lives of every man, woman, and child on this city? I'm not a gambler, and so my answer is no."

The two warriors glared at one another over the table, but their impasse continued. Eventually, Jyn stood up and rolled his shoulders back. "You know what comes next?"

Radyn nodded, hating that he did. "You'll send me back for the girl."

"You'll agree you're the perfect candidate. If the mission goes sideways, I can always claim that you were working on your own. That both of you,"—he cast a meaningful look in Nikki's direction—"far exceeded what I had originally asked you to do."

"Don't rope her into this," Radyn warned.

"You're the one that roped her in the moment Tanwen was involved. If anyone saw you leave—"

"No one saw us leave," Radyn interrupted.

"If anyone saw you leave, it'll cause even more problems for me. For better or for worse, your two fates are entwined now."

Jyn walked toward the door but stopped before pulling it open. "I want to make myself clear, so that there is no room for misunderstanding between us. You can capture and control the girl and bring her here, or you can kill her. Do either of those and my promise to you stands. I'll wipe the blood from your name. Otherwise, it's probably best if you don't return."

With that, Jyn left the building, closing the door gently behind him.

15

———

"You two really have a complicated relationship, don't you?" Nikki asked.

"Yes, but that's a conversation for another day. Right now, we need to figure out how to return to Starfall."

"Aren't we going to take Tanwen?"

The corner of Radyn's mouth turned up in a smile when he heard the hope in her voice. She'd been terrified to make the jump, and he didn't blame her for that, but she'd taken quickly to riding.

"That was my plan, but I don't know how to get you safely to the ground. Now that I have shards, I can jump off, but you can't."

Radyn led her deeper into the nest. Tanwen rested in the landing zone as though he also knew it wouldn't be long before he got to fly again. Radyn poked his head in one building after another, looking for something that would deliver Nikki secretly and safely. There had to be something the clan had created for the purpose.

Nikki followed him for a bit, then admitted. "I have a shard, too."

Radyn almost froze in mid-stride. He stopped and turned. "What? Then why are you a Shield?"

"I can connect with the shard, but if I keep the connection open for too long, I get sick. I couldn't pass the trials, but after helping the Blade with a difficult problem, he gifted me the shard as a reward. It comes in useful sometimes."

Radyn pointed at Tanwen and came close. "You should have told me! If you'd been connected when we attempted that jump, you would have been brushed away like a leaf and there's nothing I could have done."

Nikki put her hands on her hips. "I'm not a fool. I completed all the Dagger training."

Radyn figured any further lectures could wait. They'd already been on Firestone longer than he wanted. "Can you connect between the time you jump off Tanwen and when you land?"

Nikki nodded.

"Then that's one problem solved." He turned away from the buildings and strode toward Tanwen.

Macken stopped him halfway there. "You look to be in quite the hurry to leave."

"Unfortunately, I am. No time to stay and talk, as much as I'd like that. I've missed you."

Macken snorted. "Not sure I believe that, but for what it's worth, it's good to see you, too. I'm not sure what happened between you, Jyn, and Nuela, but I never believed all the stories they told about you."

Radyn clapped Macken on the shoulder. "If all goes

well, I'll see more of you soon. But for now, thanks for taking such good care of Tanwen."

"Well, don't get ahead of yourself. I still like him more than you," Macken said.

"I'm sure you do. You probably like him more than your wife some days."

Macken laughed, a deep belly laugh. "Eh, you may have the right of it, there. You two get out of here. I've got help coming before long, and best if Tanwen is back and resting before they arrive."

Radyn nodded and connected with Tanwen. The massive dragon stood and stretched, eagerness traveling through the bond they shared. Radyn climbed up the dragon swiftly, trusting Nikki could find her own way up without trouble. "Sorry, friend, it's still not going to be much of a flight."

Once Nikki was securely positioned behind Radyn, Tanwen lumbered over to the edge of the landing zone and stepped off. Radyn's stomach jumped into his throat, but he smiled as the wind whipped at his face.

Tanwen pulled up gently and circled beneath the floating cities. From below, there were massive shadows that hung in the sky, blocking the stars and moon from sight. Radyn imagined his arrival in Starfall and pushed the vision to Tanwen. The dragon returned its approval and began its slow climb.

Radyn kept a close eye on the sky above. The cities would have their own patrols in the sky tonight, though they'd be light. The assembled cities were the only ones within many miles, so the odds of attack were slim. Radyn would have been surprised if more than three or four other dragons were in the air, but he couldn't risk being discovered by any of them.

Once they were within striking distance of Starfall, Radyn turned his head so he could speak to Nikki. "Ready? It's going to happen fast."

She tightened her grip on the dragon's scales. "Do it."

That was all the approval Tanwen needed. The dragon shot straight up, powered not by its wings but by its deep connection with the Song. They climbed fast, the bottom of Starfall rapidly growing larger. Radyn sensed Tanwen's joy at the feat burning in his own chest.

As soon as they passed the observation deck, Tanwen stopped accelerating. His speed dropped quickly, bleeding off to almost nothing by the time he rose above the level of the surface.

The dragon had misjudged his distance slightly, so it gave itself one last gentle push to give Radyn and Nikki the height they needed.

They leaped as the dragon began to drop back below the level of the surface. Radyn easily cleared the protective fence. He landed and rolled, coming to his feet smoothly. A muffled thump behind him told him Nikki hadn't made the leap correctly. He spun around and ran back to her.

She had her arms wrapped around the fence and she looked to be breathing hard. He helped her over the fence while checking to ensure no one was nearby. The Gathering was on its last legs for the evening and the fields appeared to be empty. As near as he could tell, they'd been successful.

Mostly.

He laid Nikki down on the ground. "What happened?"

"Rough landing. I think I twisted my ankle and maybe cracked some ribs."

Radyn cursed softly. Fortunately, he was connected with his shards, so he put his hands against her ankle and pushed some of his strength into it. He wasn't a skilled healer, but he could help. After a minute, he stopped and leaned back. "Better?"

She rolled her ankle around and nodded. He didn't see any grimaces of pain from her, so he assumed she was telling the truth.

"Where does your chest hurt?"

She tapped her left ribs right beneath her breast.

"I'm going to heal that, too."

She nodded her agreement.

He laid his hand on her chest and repeated the process. It took longer than the ankle. It felt more like she'd cracked her ribs than bruised them, but after a long and gentle transfer of his strength, her breathing grew easier.

He stood and extended his hand. She took it and he pulled her up. "Good to go?"

She raised one finger, then stumbled a few feet away and vomited into the field. She wiped her mouth with the back of her hand and returned. "Sorry. I don't always take well to healing, either. I should be good now, though."

He walked quickly toward the nearest stairwell, and she followed.

"What's the plan?" she asked.

"Simple. We find a place to wait outside the academy

where we won't be seen. Then we wait for the Singer's messenger to appear. Markus will come out with his trusted friends and we'll follow them to the girl."

"Seems like you're missing one important detail," Nikki said.

"Do tell." They entered the nearest stairwell and descended.

"All that might lead you to the girl, but then you'll have a fair number of angry Swords and Daggers to deal with. I assume whoever is holding the girl has some, too."

Radyn shook his head. "That doesn't matter."

They reached the floor which would lead them to the main entrance of the academy. Though the city was different, the design was the same, and Radyn had to shake off the sense of familiarity he felt so as not to forget he was in enemy territory.

He had a specific corner in mind that would allow him to keep track of people entering and leaving the academy while keeping him and Nikki relatively inconspicuous. There weren't really good places to hide in the hallways, but he hoped the corner would be sufficient.

They found the corner without problem. Radyn squatted down low and was about to poke his head around the corner when Nikki tapped him on the shoulder and handed him a small handheld mirror. He extended it into the hallway that led to the main entrance.

Two Daggers were on duty, looking bored and frustrated. Radyn watched for a moment, then slowly brought the mirror back in. It was possible he was too late, but if so, there wasn't much to be done about it. He leaned close to whisper to Nikki. "Now we wait. If anyone comes down the hallway, we can go hide behind the next corner."

"Should we split up? I could watch one of the other exits."

He'd considered that but shook his head. "Better if we're together. Besides, the Singer said that he'd send a messenger, and they'd have to travel through the main gate."

She nodded and they waited. Nikki paced silently while Radyn leaned against a wall and closed his eyes. Riding Tanwen and connected with his shards ensured sufficient strength for the fights to come, but he felt the slow creeping of exhaustion through his limbs.

Once he'd handed the girl to Jyn, he might sleep for a few days straight.

He connected with the stolen shards at his wrist to sharpen his hearing. Approaching footsteps would be their best warning.

The Song of Starfall's Engine played at the edges of his awareness. He was tempted to dive in but feared that if he did, he wouldn't pay sufficient attention to his surroundings. Again, he heard the foreign note and wondered what it could be. Was Starfall at risk of falling sometime soon?

Footsteps down the main hallway pulled him out of his reverie. He opened his eyes and nodded to Nikki. They padded silently down their side hallway and hid behind the first branching corridor. Radyn extended his mirror around the corner. Less than a minute later, he saw someone in the white robes of an initiate Singer walk down the main hallway.

"They're here. We were in time," he whispered.

His sharpened hearing could make out the conversation between the Daggers and the Singer, then the soft whoosh of the door as it was opened, and the Singer admitted. Radyn gestured for Nikki to remain well hidden while he crept back to the intersection of the main hallway and the one they'd first used for cover. He crouched and extended the mirror into the main hallway.

The doors to the academy were closed and the Daggers standing guard appeared as bored as before. Radyn didn't sense that they were waiting for anything except for their duty to end. He returned the mirror to his pocket and then walked back to Nikki. "We'll wait here for them to return. I'm guessing they won't make us wait long."

His assumption was proven true a few minutes later. The door to the academy opened and Radyn heard several sets of footsteps. Once again, he crouched and used the mirror to watch the intersection. The Singer initiate led a group of Swords, including Markus. Radyn counted six warriors plus the initiate. Once they passed, he whispered their numbers to Nikki. The excitement in her eyes died. "Six? That's too many. We should return to Firestone and seek reinforcements."

"We don't have time, and unless you've forgotten, it wasn't that easy for us to get here. Even if we somehow convinced Jyn, what is he going to do? Send an armed force onto another city? His hands are tied."

"But what are we supposed to do against six shardbearers? I might be good for one, but that's it."

"That's no problem. I can fight five," Radyn said.

"Can you? I don't doubt your potential, but you've been farming for the better part of a year."

"I can fight five," Radyn repeated. He had to, so he would, and he would win. It was as simple as that.

Nikki didn't appear convinced, but it wasn't as though they had much of a choice. Either they fought, or Markus and his compatriots would capture the girl. Radyn didn't want to know what happened then. Her lips were set in a grim line, but she nodded.

"Let's find the girl and finish this, then," she said.

16

———

Following Markus and the other warriors challenged Radyn and Nikki. The late hour meant the hallways would normally have been empty, but thanks to the Gathering, there were still a handful of people wandering about, either drunk or looking for something to drink. Still, Radyn assumed that Markus and the others would know what he and Nikki looked like, so it was difficult to avoid all notice.

That was far easier said than done. A heel that came down too hard on the metal decking could easily send echoes down a hallway, and even gentle whispers tended to carry farther than they should. More than once, Radyn silently thanked Nikki for the mirror. It led the way into most new hallways, ensuring they weren't spotted inadvertently.

The only other fact in their favor was that shardbearers didn't seem concerned about being followed. And why should they? As Swords and Daggers, they were the strongest in the city. They went wherever they pleased and expected people to move aside as they strode proudly down the hallways. Why would they believe they were being hunted? In the world they inhabited, such a thing was impossible.

As Radyn witnessed their arrogance, he began to look forward to proving them wrong. Elora's guiding light had always been awareness, both of oneself and of one's surroundings. That teaching had made Radyn dangerous, but the men he hunted possessed next to none.

They dropped down several levels and went quite a way outward before the group slowed. Through the mirror, Radyn saw that the hallways were filled with scaffolding and loose sheets of metal. The scaffolding supported the hallway but also narrowed it considerably. It was only wide enough for one person to pass through at a time, and if they were broad-shouldered, they had to turn at an angle.

The group of shardbearers turned again, and Radyn and Nikki hurried after them. Radyn led the way into the scaffolding. He'd walked through repair work before, but it never ceased to amaze him. He tended to think of his city as something solid and impermeable. Seeing the hallway stripped of its walls like this was like peeling the flesh of a human back to reveal the muscle, bone, and arteries hidden beneath. The space behind the scaffolding was filled with pipes and wires, the purpose of each more mysterious to Radyn than the Song of the Engine that kept them floating in the sky.

Like seeing a child with a wound, the sight of the hallway put Radyn in a protective mood. Starfall wasn't his city, but thousands of souls called it their own. He didn't want it to fall to disaster any more than he wanted Firestone's end.

When he reached the intersection Markus and his allies had turned down, he thrust the mirror out ahead of him. Then he pulled it back slowly and handed it to Nikki. He leaned close and whispered, "They're bunched up outside a door."

She thought for a moment, then nodded. "It's a good place to hide someone. Residential quarters, but probably temporarily abandoned because of the repair work. How do you want to approach this?"

Radyn had been wondering the same. "We wait until they attempt to grab the girl. Then we attack in the confusion."

She agreed.

"You're confident you can take one?" Radyn asked. He didn't want to leave her a task she couldn't handle.

"So long as they're a Dagger. I won't last long against a Sword."

Radyn nodded. He held the stolen hilt out to her, but she shook her head. "Too many shards for me, but thanks."

He shrugged and gripped the hilt in his right hand. He connected with the shards around his wrist, basking in the sharpness and vividness of the world. Markus's allies were breathing heavily, but the fight hadn't started yet.

He listened as their maniblades punched holes through the steel where the hinges of the door would be located. Another maniblade cut down the right side of the door where the lock would be. The fourth man of the team braced himself and charged against the door.

It was the same entry technique Radyn had learned as an initiate, and this group performed it well. They could have been a bit faster. For maximum surprise, the fourth person on the team was supposed to already be charging as the maniblades cut the door free from its bindings. Either they hadn't worked together before or they weren't as experienced. Regardless, Radyn took it as a positive sign.

He turned the corner as soon as he heard the last of the footsteps rush into the room. Light streamed from the open window as the maniblades lit the space, and Radyn listened as maniblades struck one another. It was perfect. He could walk right into the middle of the chaos and take control of the situation.

Except it didn't work that way. The maniblade duels ended before Radyn was even halfway to the door. Bodies hit the floor with a heavy thud, and someone groaned in agony. Markus's familiar voice came from the open door. "Pick her up and let's get going."

Radyn hurried faster, but he still wasn't to the door by the time Markus stepped out. His eyes widened when he saw Radyn, but his surprise only lasted for a heartbeat. Then he shook his head. "I was wondering where you'd gone. Thanks for not making me search for you. I've had enough of hide-and-seek for a lifetime."

Markus already had a hilt in hand, and with a thought, the maniblade sprang to life. Radyn mirrored the action and took a step forward. He connected with the shards in his body, too. With so little room to maneuver, speed would be even more important. "What do you want with the girl?"

Markus answered with his maniblade. It leaped forward like a snake and stabbed at Radyn's chest and throat. Radyn deflected the stabs but still had to give half a step of ground to Markus. Markus strode forward, his eyes narrowed.

Markus's allies came out then. One was dripping blood from a wound on his arm, but the strongest of them had a girl thrown over her shoulder. Her body was limp and hair covered her face, but it very much looked like the girl Radyn had seen just that morning at the Gathering.

It felt as though it had been a lifetime ago.

Radyn looked around but didn't see any way of stopping them. His and Markus's duel blocked the narrow passage, and even if Nikki could get around, she couldn't do anything against five shardbearers.

The only way to save the girl was to go through Markus. Radyn didn't have a problem with that.

Markus's allies paused at the sight of the duel, but Markus gave them orders without turning around. "Get her to where she needs to go. Don't worry about me, I'll be right behind you."

The others accepted his orders and took off down the hallway.

Radyn lunged forward, but Markus deflected the cut easily. "Ask your questions now. I've got all the time in the world."

Radyn lashed out again, a combination of short cuts and quick stabs that should have at least forced Markus backward. If he could get Markus to the door he'd busted down, perhaps Nikki could sneak around.

Markus barely moved his feet. His maniblade licked at Radyn's arms and chest, and again Radyn was forced to give half a step of ground.

Markus seemed disappointed. "Is this all? I'd expected more, considering the stories that are told about you."

The fire burning in Radyn's chest doubled in size at the insult, but he kept his response controlled. He stabbed and cut, searching for an opening in Markus's defense.

Markus looked bored as he deflected the attacks. Before long, Radyn was on the defensive once again. Markus's attacks looked as lazy as his defense, but Radyn couldn't regain the offensive.

Radyn retreated another pace, and this time Markus didn't follow. He was looking at the scaffolding as if he found the repairs more interesting than the duel. A moment later, he let the maniblade in his hand vanish.

"This is pointless. Your time as a farmer has stolen your skill. Your body is tight and your movements predictable. You've avoided being cut, which I suppose is impressive enough, but there's no point in continuing. We've already got the girl, and it's clear there's nothing you can do, so promise to walk away and I'll let you live. You're nothing but a farmer now."

For a moment, Radyn wondered if Markus possessed some sense of honor or mercy. It seemed out of place with what little he knew of the man, but he knew very little.

Then he noticed the mirth in Markus's eyes and understood.

The offer had nothing to do with honor or mercy. In their short duel, he'd seen into Radyn's heart and found a victory greater than any he could win with a maniblade. If Radyn accepted the offer, Markus knew that shame would eat him up like a poison.

Radyn wanted nothing more than to wipe the overwrought look of sincerity off Markus's face, but there was only one problem:

Markus was right.

Radyn had no problem sensing Markus's attacks. His senses were as sharp as they'd ever been. But he'd lost too much of his skill with a maniblade. His muscles were tense, and his reactions were slow. Given enough time, he had no doubt he could return to the fighting condition he'd once had, but swinging a hoe wasn't the same as swinging a maniblade.

He'd been a fool to believe otherwise.

He couldn't surrender, but he also couldn't win. Markus had backed him into a corner from which there was no escape.

The tip of his maniblade fell as Markus's smirk turned into a grin. "You understand. Good. They always did say you were clever."

Radyn brought the maniblade back up. He couldn't simply give up. He connected with all his shards. Markus noticed the shift in his posture and his eyes narrowed. His body remained loose and his maniblade rested, but he was ready for Radyn's attack.

Or, at the very least, he thought he was.

Radyn leaped forward and thrust out his maniblade. He wasn't sure who was more surprised by his speed, him or Markus. It had been almost a year since he'd connected with so many shards, and though his perception kept up with the advancement, his reactions didn't.

Markus stepped to the side as his maniblade came to life again. He swiped Radyn's stab to the side, but wasn't quite quick enough to prevent the tip of Radyn's maniblade from cutting through the flesh of his left shoulder.

Radyn's satisfaction at drawing first blood was short-lived. He reacted too slowly and stopped a moment too late. Markus twisted and struck him hard with his knee. Radyn was thrown back into the scaffolding. Thankfully, he took the worst impacts against his backside and his left shoulder, but the blow dropped him to a knee.

He returned to his feet a moment later and jumped backward as Markus cut down at him. All the man's mirth and superiority had been replaced by a sneer of disdain.

Radyn retreated as Markus cut again, but the Starfall Sword didn't pursue. He swept his maniblade around in a wide vertical circle. Radyn frowned, wondering what Markus hoped to accomplish.

Then Markus took a step back and repeated the motion and Radyn understood. The scaffolding groaned like an old man getting out of bed, then screamed like a high-pitched child. Radyn retreated as metal and wood crashed between him and Markus, the ringing of pipes echoed and magnified in the tight confines of the hallway.

The mess in front of Radyn settled, but the sounds continued. Radyn caught hints of motion down the hall and assumed Markus had cut down even more of the scaffolding to cover his retreat. Radyn swore. He made a fist and was about to punch the debris but thought better of it. Markus's maniblade had left plenty of sharp-edged fragments. There was no point in making the traitorous Sword's task any easier.

He stumbled back, suddenly weary from the effort. His body was used to days in the field. Hard as they were, it was a different exhaustion from channeling the strength of the shards.

He'd lost and, in the process, had lost the girl, too.

She was in the wind, and he couldn't guess where they'd take her next.

17

R adyn should have known better. Nikki had warned him. She'd known that he wasn't enough against the forces arrayed against them, but he'd made the same mistake Elora had always warned him about. He'd spent too much time telling himself a story, and he'd lost touch with reality.

He stumbled backward and sat down. His rear hurt where it had struck the scaffolding, but the pain barely registered.

He'd spent a year pretending to be a farmer.

Pretending. Or so he'd thought.

He hadn't kept up with any form of training, not even in the privacy of his home. He'd become a farmer, from the dirt under his fingernails to the condition of his body. The shards embedded in his limbs had given him a false sense of confidence, a belief that he could become a Sword with little more than a thought.

Hadn't Nikki proven that? He could argue that she

had twisted his arm. That she and Jyn had put him in a position where he couldn't do anything but agree to help. And perhaps that was true.

But he'd been excited when she came to him. Eager to put his dormant skills to use again.

Aria had known. She'd seen him more clearly than he saw himself. She'd believed he could return, if not to being a Sword, to being one who could use the skills he'd spent years developing.

He swore again, then realized Nikki was talking to him. He rubbed his eyes and shook his head to clear his thoughts. They continued to swirl like a whirlpool, though, always ready to pull him back in if he didn't run from them.

"Sorry, I wasn't listening. What did you ask?"

She had every right to be furious at him. Perhaps, if he'd listened more closely to her, they wouldn't be in this situation. And she did sound frustrated, but she fought to keep her tone even. "What do we do now?"

"I don't know. They could take her anywhere. As clan, nobody would even think to question them."

Nikki sat down beside him. "There has to be something we're missing. Some clue we've overlooked."

Radyn tried to look back at all that had happened, but he couldn't push his memory further back than his duel with Markus.

You're just a farmer.

Markus had been right.

The snap of Nikki's fingers brought him back to the present. "Radyn, I need you here. We got this far together, but I can't do the rest alone."

"You might be better off."

"If I quit every time somebody beat me at something, I wouldn't be the Blade's right-hand Shield, would I? And somehow, I suspect you wouldn't have become a legendary Sword, either."

"But I'm not a Sword. Not anymore. I'm a farmer."

Nikki scoffed, and he shot her a hard look.

"If you think you're a farmer, then I'm the Blade of Nightkeep."

Radyn could only stare at her as though she was speaking the builder's language.

"Radyn, I have the strength of Senior Dagger when I connect to my shards, and believe me, I was connected while you two fought. I was looking for any way through that fight. Even connected to the shards, I couldn't follow your fight. And I couldn't even come close to seeing your last attack. I've never seen anyone move that fast before."

She shrugged. "I'm willing to accept that you're out of practice, and you may spend too much time in the fields, but trust me, you're no farmer. You've got a gift, just like every other shardbearer."

Her words, combined with her certainty, cracked the stone that had lodged in his chest. He swallowed hard as it crumbled into dust.

He had a gift, just like every other shardbearer. His body tensed as the hairs on the back of his arm stood up. "Why Singers?"

Nikki couldn't follow the sudden change. She gave him a questioning look.

"Why were Singers delivering the message to the academy? Why was Markus meeting with a Singer?"

"Presumably because the girl's gift has something to do with the Song."

Radyn shook his head. "That was all I thought, as well. But there must be more. Why would a Singer initiate deliver the message, especially if they felt that time mattered?"

The revelation was there. He felt it in every cell of his body. He just needed to draw it out. Another detail didn't make sense. "It's too fast. They were looking for a girl in a city. I'm sure you've had to search for missing people. How long does it take Firestone's Shields to comb the city?"

Her eyes went wide. "A week, minimum. And even then, we're lucky to find anyone trying to remain hidden. There are too many places."

"Markus knew it was going to be quick. I'm not sure about all the ways Singers are involved, but they're the ones who found the girl. And if they could, then so can I."

"You're not a Singer," Nikki replied.

"No, but I'm sensitive enough for this."

Radyn closed his eyes, connected to the shards, and listened. As before, the Song of Starfall's engine filled his mind. He ignored the Song and searched for the foreign notes he'd heard before. He couldn't hear the notes at first, but as his body relaxed and his spirit traveled deeper, he found her.

Her notes were flat and nearly silent, but he could hear them. Could place them.

He tried to hold the Song in his head as he opened his eyes and stood. "I think I can feel her. They're above us and climbing."

"Do you think they're trying to reach a bridge?"

Radyn pursed his lips, then shrugged. "I couldn't guess. It seems like carrying a body across a bridge would be hard, but maybe they have a plan. They've clearly got allies on Firestone."

He pulled Nikki to her feet, but before they left, they heard someone cough inside the room that had once sheltered the girl. Nikki met Radyn's gaze. He cast out his senses for the girl's note and found her again. It felt as though she'd stopped. Perhaps they'd only moved her to another room.

"I think we have time. Besides, if we knew more about what was happening, maybe we'd be able to stop chasing our tails."

Nikki looked like she'd been hoping for that answer. Thankfully, Radyn's last attack had forced Markus further down the hallway, so Radyn only had to cut through a bit of broken scaffolding to reach the open door.

The scene almost made him sick. Two young men had been butchered with maniblades. Limbs and blood covered the deck. There were cuts in the deck, too, which matched what Radyn had heard from the hallway. The defenders had been killed, but after they'd fallen, their attackers had cut them up like cattle.

The senselessness of it shook him to his core. Battle was brutal and violent, but this was something else, something darker.

Another cough raised his eyes to a bed. An older woman sat there, holding her hand to her side. She'd been cut, too, and her face was pale, but she was sitting up and watching him. Radyn rushed to her. She flinched back.

"You don't need to worry. I can heal you a little."

She looked at him for a moment, then nodded. She lifted her hand. She'd been cut on the left side of her stomach, but when Radyn pulled aside the fabric of her tunic, the cut didn't look too deep. If he could close the cut, she should live until she could find a better healer.

He pressed his hand against her side. He was already connected to the shards, so all he needed to do was push some of his strength into her side. Her flesh grew warm to the touch as it stitched itself back together. The effort took more strength than he'd imagined, but he'd never had much skill at healing.

When it was over, he lifted his hand. Some of the wound remained, but it was nothing more than a small cut now. She shouldn't be at risk of bleeding out.

Nikki led with the questions. "Who is the girl and why is she so important?"

The older woman met Nikki's glare with a calm gaze. "Why do you want to know?"

"I'm a Shield from Firestone. It was one of our Daggers that was killed in Robyn's home. As near as we can tell, our Dagger tortured and killed Robyn, but then one of your people killed our Dagger."

The woman grunted. "Impressive."

Nikki ignored the compliment. "I can't say I'm too saddened about the death of a Dagger as wicked as ours was, but the girl's at the heart of it, and my partner and I think those that just took her have more planned."

Radyn's chest warmed when Nikki described him as her partner, but the older woman was less impressed. She looked between the two of them, then sighed. "I'm afraid you're right, though I don't know how you put so much together. We also don't know what they want with the girl, but her potential is beyond anything we've seen. I wouldn't be surprised if they attempted to bring a city down."

Radyn fought the urge to stick his finger in his ear and clear out the wax, because he was certain he hadn't heard her correctly. "Did you say, 'bring a city down?'"

The woman nodded, and there was no hint of madness in her gaze.

"Why would anyone want to bring a city down?" Radyn asked.

"We don't know for sure. It could be that they just crave the power over other cities. There are those among us who suspect other motives, though. Their actions horrify us. You can see it for yourself here. They don't just kill, they slaughter."

"And what about you?" Nikki asked. "You took the girl, most likely by force. You didn't turn her in to the Shields or the Swords that were looking for her. How are you any better?"

The woman flinched from the words but didn't deny Nikki's accusations. She pointed to one of the corpses. "He was the one who kidnapped Kaya. We learned a girl had appeared mysteriously in the Engine room and then disappeared. He'd been searching for her and found her at the Gathering."

She wiped away a tear that had formed at the corner of her eyes. "He'd always been sensitive to the Song. Someday, he might have been a great Singer. He felt her and followed her at a distance. When she entered Robyn's home, he followed her to the door, hoping to introduce himself. He heard a shout and a struggle and followed behind. He came upon the Dagger from Firestone in the process of kidnapping her."

The woman paused and glanced at the corpse. She smiled softly, pride and sorrow mixing in equal parts as she looked upon the young man. Radyn wondered if she was his mother. Her affection seemed too powerful to be a mere compatriot.

She resumed, "He killed the Dagger but didn't know what to do. He didn't dare leave the girl, not after seeing what had happened to Robyn. So, he picked her up and brought her here. Perhaps it was a mistake, and he certainly brought her without her permission, but it was with the best intent."

Nikki's retort was sharp. "I wonder if those who killed Robyn and your friend believed the same."

The woman's face fell.

"You still didn't answer what you hoped to achieve by having her," Radyn said.

The woman nodded and looked up again, her gaze traveling between them, weighing them on some scale Radyn couldn't perceive. Considering her circumstances, he was surprised by her indecision.

"I'm part of a group that seeks to return humans to the surface in large numbers. You might not know this, but there are Engines buried down in the surface and we need someone who has the ability to bring them back to life. Kaya might just be that person. We had hoped she might be willing to come with us when we left," the older woman said.

"Don't you think that would be a decision for her parents?" Radyn asked.

The woman's gaze was sharp. "Her Father is a Singer for Nightkeep. He's among the leaders of the movement we're struggling against. He's hunting for her, but not because he loves her. She ran away from him in the first place."

"You're certain of this?" Nikki asked.

The woman nodded. "It would be a loss for us if she didn't want to join us, but we'd respect her decision. But you have to ensure her father doesn't find her."

Nikki met Radyn's gaze, silently questioning him. Radyn shrugged. The reasons behind everything had ceased to matter as much to him. He'd watched Markus and his allies carry the unconscious girl away. He wouldn't rest until she was safe. "I'm going after them."

"Not without me," Nikki said.

"What about her?" Radyn asked.

"I can always find her again. The girl is more important."

Radyn checked to ensure the stolen hilt was secured and the shards were pressed tightly against his wrist. Despite Nikki's reassurances, doubt remained. Once, he would have advanced without fear. Now, after almost a year in the fields, he wasn't sure if he possessed the skills necessary to beat Markus and those with him. He stared at the stolen band with its shards.

What did it matter? If he walked away now, he'd never live with himself. He was as ready as he would ever be. He looked at Nikki and tried to project a confidence he wished he felt. "Then let's find her."

18

Kaya fought and clawed her way back to awareness one exhausting inch at a time. Her body felt heavy, and the sickly-sweet smell from the hood lingered in her nose. She felt herself being carried, the person moving her unconcerned with her comfort. He'd tossed her over his shoulder, and more than once, that shoulder drove deep into her stomach.

She tried to move her limbs but couldn't succeed at anything more than convincing her fingers to twitch. The people who had kidnapped her had forced her to sleep and were moving her again. Her heart beat a bit stronger at the realization, but the drug gripped her tightly in its sleepy embrace.

There was nothing she could do, but she took comfort in believing they didn't know she was stirring. Asleep, she was helpless, but once she could focus, she could teach them they'd made a mistake.

She tried to keep track of the twists, turns, and stairs they took, but her weary mind couldn't keep hold of the memories. She drifted in and out of sleep, never reaching full awareness. There were stairs and hallways, but they only registered as brief impressions.

Finally, the journey came to a brief but very welcome respite. The man who'd been carrying her laid her down on a table. She let her body flop as naturally as she could, but she heard someone say, "It looks like she's waking up."

Shadowy figures moved around her, but she couldn't keep her eyes open for more than a moment. She stretched out on the table and tried to get comfortable.

"If she wakes, she wakes, though hopefully, we can be off this city before she's truly up." This voice was deeper and more authoritative than the first.

"How long until everything is ready?" the first voice asked.

"Not long. Our allies are clearing the way. Go stand guard. I don't think we'll have any more problems, but I won't underestimate Radyn."

She heard the shuffling of feet, the opening of a door, and then a weight settling in a chair. Then, blissful silence, and she felt herself drifting off again. She slipped into a peaceful darkness.

When she woke, she wasn't sure how much time had passed. It might have been a few minutes, or it might have been a few hours. She kept her eyes closed as bodies shuffled around. "We're ready," a new voice said.

"Perfect timing. She woke up a minute ago," the deep voice said.

Kaya opened her eyes and saw the faces of her captors, then frowned. These weren't the same ones as before. The woman was gone, replaced by a man with steely gray hair and eyes that seemed hollow. He looked like a man who had seen terrible sights, and the longer he looked in her direction, the more convinced she was that he had been the cause of much of that terror.

Her blood froze when he smiled. "Welcome, Kaya, daughter of Linden. We've been searching for you for many days now."

Her thoughts hadn't yet caught up with her surroundings. How did this man know who her father was?

"Where are you taking me?" Kaya asked.

"Someplace where you'll be safe," the man said.

From anyone else, she might have found the assurance comforting. Coming from this man, the words unsettled her. Instinctively, she didn't trust him. As her thoughts and senses finally stirred to life, she noticed something else about him. He was a Singer, though not one she recognized. The Song of Starfall's Engine wrapped around him, even though he seemed blind to the fact.

She wanted to run and hide, but there was no place for her to run to. This room was small and there were guards at the door. Now that she could hear the Song, she knew she was close to the surface and perhaps halfway between the edge of the city and Engine. She vaguely remembered climbing, so they were taking her closer to the surface. "You didn't answer my question. Where are you taking me?"

The man ignored her. He stood and gestured to the others, launching a flurry of activity in the small space.

She didn't want to be with these men. They frightened her.

But what could she do? She was one young woman against at least three men. She wasn't helpless but didn't think she was strong enough to escape.

As she always did, she turned to the Song for guidance. It spoke true even when lies surrounded her. The Song filled her head with its music. The Engine was the loudest, but there were other parts playing, too. The man she'd seen at the Gathering, the one the Song had carried her toward, now ran toward her.

The men who kept her captive didn't give him the time to reach them, though. As soon as they were prepared, they filed out, and the gray-haired man gestured her forward.

She thought she should fight and delay, but she feared they would put another bag over her head, and she'd end up asleep while they carried her while they pleased. The only fight she could muster was to shuffle forward instead of hurrying to obey.

"Faster, girl. Your father is eager to be reunited with his precious daughter."

Her eyes shot up. The man realized, a moment too late, the slip of his tongue. The thought of being returned to Father gave her the strength to push past her fear. Only the gray-haired man stood between her and freedom and the Song strengthened her legs. She darted past him as he tried to close his hand around her wrist. In one move, she was past him, and then she ran down the hallway as fast as her legs could carry her.

Several pairs of footsteps followed her, every bit as

fast as she was. She took a corner at random, but her pursuit was right behind her.

Her lungs ached and her legs burned, but she pushed harder, ignoring the pain. A set of stairs was coming up on her left. She cut toward them and ran down the flight, taking the steps three at a time. She feared missing a step and crashing down, and she hit the bottom of the flight with a sense of relief.

It didn't last long. The footsteps behind her went silent, but before she realized the danger she was in, a foot connected with her shoulder. The kick sent her flying into the wall. One of the younger men who'd been guarding the door stood over her, a slight sheen of sweat on his forehead. She tried to scramble to her feet, but as soon as she put her hand on the ground to lever herself up, she screamed. Fire burned all the way up her arm, forcing tears from her eyes.

She used her left hand, but before she could reach her feet, the young man, who had to at least be a Dagger, drove his fist hard into her stomach. She doubled over as all the breath left her body. He picked her up as though she was nothing more than a bag of potatoes he had to carry to the kitchen. Once again, she was thrown over his shoulder, and he walked in such a way that he drove his shoulder regularly into her stomach.

Soon, she stood before the gray-haired man. He grabbed her under the chin and yanked her face up as he bent down so she had no choice but to stare into his hollow eyes. "Try to do anything like that again and there will be severe consequences."

He let go and stood up, then slapped her hard across

the face. The slap stung, but the surprise hurt worse. He met her tear-filled gaze. "Much worse," he threatened.

The group surrounded her, leaving her no options to escape. Together, they went toward the nearest stairwell and climbed. Whenever Kaya dragged her feet, one of the men behind her would shove her roughly forward.

She'd had one chance, and she'd failed.

The small party emerged on the surface of the city. Kaya hadn't held out much hope that the city Shields would help, but they were nowhere to be found. The night was either very late or the morning very early, and the Gathering was silent. Everyone was in bed, either theirs or someone else's, and no last revelers remained.

The gray-haired man led them straight across the fields. Kaya's feet slipped and her ankles twisted as she stumbled through the uneven soil of the harvested fields. Clouds above the city blocked the stars and moon from sight. They marched toward a distant pair of lanterns, but Kaya couldn't tell if they were bridges or some other structure.

She listened to the Song, which revealed the truth. Dragons waited ahead. They took her toward Starfall's nest.

She tried to run again, but muscular arms reinforced with the strength of shards stopped her easily. The gray-haired man cuffed her across the side of the head, leaving her dizzy. She half stumbled, half was pulled closer to the lanterns.

They stopped too soon, and their leader gestured to one of the small shacks they passed. Kaya knew them well enough from when she'd gone to the surface of

Nightkeep with Father. They were scattered across the surface to store the tools that the farmers needed to work the fields. Somehow, she didn't think they were looking for digging forks.

Sure enough, two of the men soon came back carrying a large chest between them. They moved quickly, though, which led Kaya to think the chest was empty. A sinking feeling settled in her stomach. It solidified into a stone when they set the crate down in front of her and opened the lid to reveal what appeared to be a yawning abyss.

"Get in," the leader said.

Kaya shook her head and took a step back, but she'd exhausted her captors' patience. The man gestured with his finger and the same Dagger that had carried her earlier stepped forward and delivered another well-placed punch before she could flinch away. As before, she crumpled, and the Dagger picked her up and stuffed her in the chest. They pushed her arms tight in and folded her legs until she was almost in the fetal position. Then the lid slammed shut.

"Scream if you want, but it won't matter," she heard the gray-haired man say from outside the chest. "You're only in the chest, so the dragon can carry you more easily. The guards at the nest already know we're coming."

Kaya wasn't sure she could even scream if she wanted to. It was all she could do to breathe. She'd never been in such a tight space before. She couldn't expand her lungs and take a deep breath even if she wanted to.

The cool night air of the surface quickly became a distant memory. They hadn't been kind enough to drill any air holes in the chest. The air grew warm and stale with her own breath. Her heart pounded in her chest. The motion of her cage made her queasy. Slight motions felt like they were tossing her around. It felt as though the darkness swirled around her.

Instinctively, she listened for the Song, but it sounded like it never had before. It pounded in her ears as though it beat in time with her heart. She tried to soothe it, tried to let it know that everything would be fine.

But the Song saw into her as clearly as she saw into it, and it wasn't fooled by her lies. It sounded a discordant note, and she heard the tremor of the city through the walls of the chest. The motion that sickened her stopped.

"What was that?" asked one of the men.

"Don't stop, you fools! We need to hurry." If not for her circumstances, Kaya might have smiled at the fear in his voice.

The movement in the chest worsened as she was tossed from side to side. She hadn't eaten since that morning, but she felt the food and acid working its way up through her stomach and into her throat. She searched for anything that would distract her. Anything that would take her away, however briefly, from the sheer terror of her confinement.

She heard him coming, running up toward the surface. He was louder now to her sense, a beacon in the perfect darkness she endured.

Another pressure grew, layered on top of the pressing nature of the chest. She recognized this feeling, too, a melody she hadn't heard in a long time. Father had noticed when she visited the surface how the dragons reacted to her presence. He'd pushed her closer until the Sword in charge of the nest had pleaded for him to back off.

She'd always loved dragons, but they didn't seem to love her in return. With every step, the Daggers carried her closer to the nest, the greater the pressure the dragons exerted on her. The Daggers felt it as well as she did. They grunted as the box became heavier to move.

Kaya scratched at the walls of her new cage, but her feeble attempts did nothing but tear away the tips of her fingernails. She gasped for a full breath that would never come, her body too compressed. The chest jerked to a sudden stop as the pressure from the dragons doubled in intensity. It felt as though she was being crushed by stones.

Unable to move.

Unable to breathe.

Her spirit broke, and the world shook in response.

19

———————

Radyn and Nikki were near the top of the stairs when the first tremble of distress passed through Starfall. The stairs shook under their feet, and Radyn considered himself fortunate that he didn't twist his ankle. He dove up the last remaining stairs, landing and rolling across the surface. By the time he reached his feet, the trembling had stopped.

When he closed his eyes, he was back in Firestone's Engine room on that fateful day so many years ago. Today, the residents who remembered it called it "The Little Fall," but it remained the memory that haunted his nightmares more often than any battle he'd ever fought.

Radyn took a deep breath as his heart threatened to beat its way out of his chest. The lights in the stairwell hadn't flickered. There had been no darkness, no everlasting moment of weightlessness.

Starfall hadn't fallen.

It couldn't fall.

If he repeated that often enough, he might even come to believe it. Nikki came up behind him, but she didn't sound nearly as scared as he thought she should be. "What was that?"

He pointed to a set of dark shadows in the distance. He'd been connected to his shards as he climbed the stairs, so he'd felt everything. "It's the girl. I think the Engine is responding to her distress."

"Then we should get to her quick." As good as her word, Nikki took off at a sprint.

With the shards banishing his exhaustion and strengthening his limbs, Radyn had no problem catching up and running beside her. He ran lightly across the fields, the wind refreshing against his face. He soon outpaced Nikki but didn't let himself get too far in front of her. The enemy shardbearers wouldn't fall without help.

As they neared, Radyn made their opponents out clearly. Two Daggers carried a chest that should have held tools from the fields. Now, though, it felt as though a Singer screeched discordant notes at the Engine from within. Radyn couldn't tell if the girl's song was intentional or if it was a panicked response to her captivity.

Either way, he needed to free her.

Their destination was apparent. They made a straight line toward the nest, led by the gray-haired Singer Markus had met with in the grove. Two other shardbearers and Markus formed a loose ring of protection around the others. They weren't too far from the nest, but the Daggers appeared to be struggling to carry the weight.

It was no wonder. If the girl sang, the pressure of the dragons would fight them every step of the way. They would never get to the nest if they didn't do something about her.

The Singer leading them seemed to realize it, too. He turned and stopped the chest suddenly.

Several things happened at once. The Singer noticed Radyn and Nikki approaching, and his eyes went wide as his hand came up to point at them. Heads turned and hands went to maniblades. Radyn reached down for his, but before he could, he heard the scream.

It wasn't a sound, but it rang in his head and chest like a bell. It came from the girl, and the Engine reacted. The massive stone howled like a wounded animal, so loud it forced Radyn to clap his hands over his ears.

His reaction did nothing. The screams of agony and dismay weren't heard by his ears but experienced by his spirit. His legs threatened to collapse, but still, he stumbled forward.

He made it a step before Starfall reacted. The surface of the city tipped, reminding Radyn once again that they lived on a mountain that floated in the sky. Like a top slowing to a stop, the land tilted. Off in the distance, the bridges that Radyn and the others had worked so hard to build collapsed, metal squealing as loud booms signaled the cracking of the anchors.

Radyn fell to the side and dug his hands deep into the soft soil of the fields. He kicked his toes into the dirt, creating impromptu hand and foot holds. The surface tilted even further, and Radyn pressed himself tight into the ground. Beside him, Nikki did the same. A small log from a felled tree barreled toward them, forcing Radyn to scamper to the side. It careened further down the slope, eager to flatten whatever stood in its way.

The city groaned under the unusual stresses. Metal and stone bent and buckled under loads they were never designed to bear. The city began to right itself, and Radyn pushed himself to his feet. He spared a moment to look in the direction of the bridge. He couldn't see Firestone from where he stood, and all he could do was hope it hadn't suffered the same fate as Starfall.

He helped Nikki to her feet, then resumed the chase. One of the shardbearers who'd been escorting the chest had tumbled a few feet away before anchoring himself to the ground, but the others remained roughly where they'd been before. The Daggers responsible for carrying the chest had made sure it didn't drop away. When they saw Radyn and Nikki approaching, they tried to pull it closer to the nest, but it wouldn't budge.

Radyn wasn't surprised. Kaya's Song was nearly as loud as the Engine's. He was surprised that the Singer, even disconnected from his shards, couldn't hear it. It wouldn't be long, though, before he took action to silence the girl.

Indeed, the Singer gestured for the two Daggers to throw open the lid of the chest as Radyn drew closer. They moved to do so, but Radyn lost sight of them as Markus and the other shardbearers stepped in his path.

Markus smirked as he pointed in the direction Radyn had come from. "The fields are that way, farmer."

Radyn heard the insult, but the words didn't stab into him the way they had before. Kaya had proven beyond a shadow of a doubt that she could manipulate the Engine by herself, and he'd made a promise to Aria that she would never be forced to endure the failure of another Engine.

He'd die before failing to keep that promise.

Radyn's stolen maniblade came to life. The strength of all his shards, stolen and personal, flowed through his limbs and sharpened his perception. Even in the dark, he caught the subtle shift of Markus's weight. They passed, and this time Markus's maniblade never came close. Radyn deflected it off its line.

He didn't turn to continue his duel with Markus. Instead, he turned his attention to one of the two shardbearers standing behind the Sword. The shardbearer's maniblade appeared in hand, but when lit, it wasn't much longer than the length of a short sword. Radyn's greater speed and maniblade length ended the contest in a single pass.

He turned to face the second of the shardbearers but was distracted by a second unnatural scream from the girl. The horror of the first scream repeated, but this time, the city tilted in the other direction. A deep shudder passed through the city, and for a moment, Radyn feared the entire mountain was about to break in pieces, torn asunder by forces no one could comprehend.

The second shardbearer stumbled backward and Markus dropped to the ground, driving his maniblade deep into the soil and twisting it to serve as an anchor.

Radyn leaped at the second shardbearer. The young

man couldn't decide whether the tilting city or the farmer was the greatest threat, and Radyn cut him down as he passed by. His leap took him much farther than he anticipated, but he dug his feet into the soil and followed Markus's example. He stabbed his maniblade into the ground and came to a stop.

The girl's scream ended with a violent blow from the Singer. Starfall slowly righted itself.

Radyn couldn't imagine the toll in lives and damage. He'd wandered the halls of Whitehawk after the collapse, and it was as though he'd walked through an endless nightmare. That city had been destroyed, but he wouldn't be surprised if the damage to Starfall was every bit as severe.

He sprinted toward the chest, but Markus intercepted him before he made it halfway. Their maniblades met again, crossing under the moonless sky. Radyn retreated, not because Markus had forced him to, but because he heard Nikki behind him. "Rescue the girl!" he shouted.

Nikki shifted direction and Markus tried to block her, but this time, Radyn stopped him. The Sword shot him a distasteful look but didn't spend too much energy attempting to pursue Nikki.

Markus settled into an unfamiliar stance, raising his maniblade to the height of his head but keeping it roughly parallel to the ground. "They told me you defeated some of Nightkeep's best Swords. Have you found some of that strength again?"

Radyn raised his own maniblade. Markus didn't need to win the duel. If he simply kept Radyn tied up here, the others would likely escape. Nikki might defeat the two remaining Daggers, but Radyn didn't want to bet the fate of a city on it.

He glared at the Sword. "Your actions tonight have likely killed dozens, if not hundreds, of innocent civilians. Why not just leave the girl alone?"

Markus shrugged. "With that kind of power, the girl was never going to be left alone. And who cares about a few lives tonight? They're only a fraction of what's to come."

Radyn didn't have a clue what that meant, but he couldn't wait any longer. One Dagger had put down the chest so that he could fight Nikki, and now the Singer and the remaining Dagger were nearing the entrance of the nest. The Singer was already calling for help from the clan at the gate.

He sprang forward, but Markus was ready. Their maniblades clashed, broke apart, then clashed again. When Radyn came too close, Markus danced nimbly back, forcing Radyn to break his defense again. Radyn pursued, but it wasn't fast enough. He could see the duel developing between Nikki and the Dagger, and Nikki wasn't winning. She might have the strength of a Senior Dagger, but she didn't have the experience.

In that way, it wasn't much different than Radyn's battle against Markus. He was faster and stronger but out of practice. Markus lacked all of Radyn's gifts, but he was a Sword who trained every day.

Radyn took a deep breath and allowed his spirit to settle. Elora's training still lived in him, not forgotten but simply put aside for a time. He expanded his attention and let it settle on Markus.

On the surface, the man appeared confident, but Radyn saw other signs. The tip of his maniblade dipped and wobbled. His eyes darted behind him as though he feared the Singer wouldn't make it to the nest.

A sense of peace fell over Radyn. He could see everything. He stepped forward, slowly at first, then fast. Markus reacted, launching his attack before Radyn could strike. Radyn saw the tension in his form a moment before he struck and was already sliding to the side. Markus twisted and followed Radyn's movement, but Radyn raised his maniblade and let the strike brush across it. He twisted his wrists and turned the deflection into a cut. Markus did the same, but Radyn was faster. His maniblade cut into Markus's unprotected side.

The maniblade didn't make it far before Markus stopped it.

Radyn stepped back. The cut was a fatal one but a slow one. Markus should have let it finish and saved himself the agony.

Markus looked down at his wound, then snarled. He took a step forward as though to pursue Radyn but was stopped by the pain. He groaned and his eyes watered.

Radyn kept his maniblade in front of him. "Why do you want the girl?"

When it was clear Markus wasn't going to answer, Radyn stepped to the side to pass him. If he ended this madness quickly enough, they might be able to keep Markus alive to answer questions.

"Rot on the other side of the gate with everyone else," Markus said.

He lurched forward faster than Radyn would have expected possible with his wound.

Radyn snapped his maniblade around, knocking Markus's aside without problem. But Markus persisted, and Radyn stepped into the hole in his defense to stab him deep in the chest.

Markus grunted. When he spoke, his words came slowly, as though he had to push them around the Sword. "You should have stayed a farmer. You would have enjoyed your last days more."

Radyn shook his head.

Markus spit at him as he died, but when Radyn let his maniblade disappear, the Sword collapsed in a heap.

He looked up. Nikki and the Dagger remained in a heated duel, so he sprinted toward them. The Dagger glanced his way as he approached, and Nikki used the distraction as an opportunity to deliver a fatal cut across his neck.

Radyn ran past the finished duel without stopping. The gates of the nest had opened, and a full squad of clan guarded the opening as the Dagger and the Singer stepped through.

Radyn shouted as the doors closed behind the fleeing criminals. He took a few more steps, then stopped. He let the connection to his shards drop so that his body could enjoy a respite. Exhaustion crashed over him, nearly bringing him to his knees. He bent over and put his hands on his thighs, breathing hard.

Nikki stopped beside him. "What happened?"

He pointed toward the nest, now sealed with guards on the walls with bows ready. Despite the turmoil of the past few minutes, they looked calm and ready. For all Radyn knew, the Singer was in there right now, claiming Radyn had caused the destruction.

He took a deep breath and stood up straight. He shook his head. "We were too late. They've got the girl and dragons."

20

———

Radyn stared at the wall of the nest and considered the possibilities. None ended well. If he wasn't made into a pincushion by the archers, he'd still have to contend with the warriors within. He guessed the others would hop on a dragon and fly to one of Nightkeep's cities. They already counted one of Starfall's Singers and Senior Swords among their number, so it wasn't hard to believe they'd have a similar level of support in Nightkeep. If what the woman below had said was true, they'd likely be taking Kaya back to her father.

Once Kaya reached Nightkeep, there was nothing else he could do. Especially after tonight. It wasn't hard to imagine the blame for tonight's events being laid squarely on him. He wouldn't be able to leave his home without a shardbearer attempting to kill him. And that was if Jyn was even willing to let him return to Firestone.

If he couldn't reach her here or there, it only left the space between.

He connected to his shards, grateful they banished

the exhaustion from his limbs. He was out of condition. Once, he'd been able to remain fully connected for almost a full day. Now, only a few minutes of combat took everything from him. When this was over, he'd want to sleep for the better part of a week.

Through his shards he called to Tanwen. The dragon eagerly responded, not satisfied with the short flights from earlier.

Then he turned to speak with Nikki. "I'm going to go after her."

"Then I'll join you."

Radyn snorted and the corner of his mouth turned up in a smile. "I appreciate your willingness to help, but this is as far as we go together."

Nikki started to object, but then she looked into his face and saw something there that stopped her in her tracks. "Why?"

Radyn looked down at his hands. "I'm more grateful than you know for everything that's happened today. But I can't fight on a dragon while worrying about you, too. Not to mention there's a damn good chance I end up starting a war between the cities. I've already been exiled in my own city, so there's not as much for me to lose. There's no reason to drag you down with me."

"You could always not start a war between the cities," Nikki said.

Radyn shook his head. Thankfully, the surface of Starfall was quiet, but he couldn't imagine the chaos happening deep below his feet. "You've experienced firsthand what she's capable of, and I get the distinct sense the men who took her don't plan on using that strength for anything we'd approve of. It needs to be stopped, regardless of the consequences."

She pressed her lips tightly together, thought for a moment, then nodded. "Is there anything I can do?"

"Find the woman from below. She still knows more than we do, and it'll be good to get her to Firestone once all of this is over. If you can, return to the place where we first hopped on Tanwen. Assuming I'm successful, I'll come back and pick everybody up on my way to Firestone."

"Good luck."

"You, too."

With that, Radyn ran toward the edge of the city, away from the nest. A few shouts from the walls followed him, but soon, he would be lost to the darkness. He ignored the voices, thinking only of how he might reach Kaya before it was too late.

He sensed Tanwen's delight through their connection. Radyn imagined that poor Macken was red in the face from shouting, but it wouldn't matter to Tanwen. The dragon was in the air and rapidly approaching the same point Radyn ran toward.

Radyn leaped over the fence with an easy step, then jumped straight off the edge of the city.

He basked in the brief feeling of flight, then landed on Tanwen's broad back a moment later. The dragon had flown closer to the surface than Radyn had expected, but he was grateful for the softer landing. He climbed quickly to Tanwen's neck and positioned himself in his typical seat.

It was strange. Before today, he hadn't ridden on

Tanwen in almost a year, but it felt in a way as though he was returning home after a long day in the fields.

Like he belonged.

Tanwen dropped altitude as Radyn got into place. He looked up, but in the cloudy sky, he couldn't spot his enemies. He gripped Tanwen's scales tightly and closed his eyes to better focus on the Song. Kaya's presence wasn't as obvious as it had been when she'd been conscious, but with Tanwen aiding his senses, he found her. She was starting to move. The dragon carrying her began its flight.

He urged Tanwen higher, and Tanwen eagerly agreed. They shot up toward Starfall, the enormous city looming over them like an oversized, broken top. Tanwen flew them close to the walls of the city to protect them from discovery. Most dragons flew with their heads down and eyes pointed at the ground. It was an evolutionary pattern developed to help them hunt.

In this age, it helped prevent the exact type of attack Radyn hoped to use. The underside of the dragons' necks was one of their most vulnerable locations. If Tanwen could latch his powerful jaws on a dragon's throat the battle was as good as won. The city that had hunted Radyn all day and night now served as his protection.

A dragon took off from the city. It dove as Radyn and Tanwen rose, and only Tanwen's quick reflexes saved them from a midair collision that would have broken both dragons.

The other rider shouted as they passed, and Radyn recognized the last Dagger who had helped carry the chest.

Tanwen and Radyn reacted as one. Tanwen brought his ascent to a screeching halt, almost throwing Radyn off in the process. Radyn held on tight as his stomach tried to find its way outside his body through a crack in his spine.

Tanwen dove, folding in his wings and shoving himself downward, revealing a mastery of the Song Radyn had never had the time to explore. They sped toward the surface of the world below as if launched from the world's largest bow.

The other dragon's flight remained erratic as it fought to recover from the near collision. The Dagger looked up to the sky, searching for an attacker he hadn't expected. By the time he spotted Tanwen falling, it was too late. Tanwen asked Radyn for permission, which Radyn granted without hesitation.

The movement of Tanwen's jaws was so quick that Radyn barely felt the reach. But he shared senses with the dragon, so he knew when Tanwen's jaws closed over the helpless Dagger and snatched him from his mount.

For a moment, Radyn swore he could taste the blood and bone in his own mouth, but the sensation passed as he directed Tanwen higher into the sky. Kaya was already almost halfway to Nightkeep.

They shot up and at an angle, searching for any sign of the dragon or its precious cargo. The cloud cover lightened for a moment, brightening the sky just enough for Radyn to spot the shadow overhead. He urged Tanwen on. The dragon, having just enjoyed a snack, was more than eager.

The Starfall dragon saw them coming and banked

away. As it did, Radyn saw the chest clutched in its claws. He and Tanwen followed the dragon and rider.

He hadn't thought his plan through well enough. Any attack on the dragon risked Kaya's life. He could all too easily imagine the chest being dropped or crushed in the middle of a battle. He wouldn't risk her life any more than was necessary.

Unfortunately, he didn't have much time. The dragon and rider had realized Radyn's predicament and hurried to Nightkeep. Tanwen kept pace, but their prey would land safely within a few minutes.

Unlike before, when she'd been under the influence of the substance in the hood, Kaya awoke with a start. She stretched, only to find she couldn't move.

Memories returned a moment later and she stifled a sob. She had sung to the Engine, and it had answered. The gray-haired man had thrown open the chest, cocked his fist back, and everything after was darkness. The side of her head throbbed.

Before she could bring her hand to her face, the chest shifted suddenly, and she was pressed even tighter against its walls. Her weight was on her head and neck, and it was all she could do to keep her neck straight.

Then the chest straightened out, easing her agony a little.

That hadn't been from the Daggers carrying her. She reached for the Song, only to find her way to it was blocked.

She was in the clutches of a dragon. Its presence prevented her from hearing the sweet melodies of the Engine. It was the first time in as long as she could remember that it hadn't been there for her.

That was the worst punishment of all, even worse than being stuffed into the chest as though she was nothing more than a gardening implement.

A growl began in the back of her throat, and she clenched her fists. Since escaping Father, she'd been hungry, hurt, and lonely, but she'd been able to endure it all because she the Song was there, guiding her the way her father should have.

They couldn't take that from her.

The fact she couldn't hear the Song didn't mean it wasn't there. She'd never challenged a dragon before, but what better time than now?

Kaya pushed aside the pain in her limbs and the shortness of her breath. The suffering of the past was in the past, and the future was still unwritten. Only the Song mattered. She heard it, whispering softly like a frightened child hiding in the middle of a cheering crowd. She pushed through the noise, focusing only on the familiar tune. It grew clearer, ringing like a single bell on a cold night.

The chest vibrated as the dragon carrying her roared its displeasure. The Song grew fainter as the noise of the crowd doubled, but she didn't let go of the sound. The dragon could roar and shake her cage, but it couldn't drown out the Song. She and it were connected. They always had been and always would, until the very end of days.

Kaya and the dragon dueled, but the dragon had never been challenged in this way. Its connection to the Song was natural, a birthright it had never questioned. It hadn't spent its entire life seeking the Song and trying to better understand it.

As Kaya's connection grew, the dragon's faded. As it lost the connection to the Song, its flight started to fail. She felt its desperation in its roar, but the Song was closer than ever, even if it was the Song of Nightkeep's Engine.

She would never go back.

The dragon fought for control, but Kaya felt her body lighten within the chest. They were falling.

She heard a shout, and then the chest split open as the dragon ripped it in two.

Kaya didn't even scream as she plummeted to the surface. She was free and with the Song, and that was all that mattered.

Radyn didn't understand the sights before him. At first, he'd been certain the dragon would reach Nightkeep without interference. But then its flight became erratic, and the dragon struggled to remain in the air.

Tanwen crept closer, but there was still little that Radyn could do.

Then, the dragon dropped several feet before righting itself. It looked as though it was about to fall again, and then it roared, flexed its powerful muscles, and ripped the chest in two. Kaya's thin form tumbled down into the darkness below. The moment she was free, the dragon from Starfall flew without problem.

Radyn sent Tanwen after the girl. The enormous dragon folded his wings and dropped, catching up to her in no time at all.

They were only a few dozen feet away when Tanwen's descent slowed. Radyn didn't have to ask why. He sensed the pressure coming from her, as strong as though it had come from an elder dragon.

He hadn't realized humans were capable of such strength, and here it was, bound to a young woman still years younger than him.

Tanwen paced Kaya as she fell. Radyn felt the dragon strain and push, but he couldn't close the gap.

Radyn maneuvered Tanwen, so they fell a little ahead of Kaya. Her gaze turned to him and he shouted, "You have to let go!"

Falling was a dream. Wind whipped past her hair, and though the surface rushed at her like a charging bull, she felt no fear. How could she, when she held onto the Song so tightly? It would carry her to the gate and maybe even beyond.

She thought of the mother she'd never met, the one who had died to give her life.

Perhaps it was time for them to meet.

There was a new note in the Song, or rather, a familiar one she'd been hearing for the past day. She twisted and there he was, not shopping for gems with his partner, but plummeting straight down on the back of a dragon.

He'd seemed content at the Gathering, but he hadn't glowed against her senses the way he did now. He shouted something, but it was lost to the roar of the wind.

She smiled, hoping he would break away before it was too late. She didn't want to take anyone to the gate with her.

He shouted again, louder than before. His voice carried, reinforced by the dragon he rode and their connection to the Song.

"Let go!"

The fool. She wasn't holding onto anything except the Song.

A moment later, she understood.

He wanted her to give up the Song. To surrender the only thing in the world that had ever given her comfort.

She shook her head.

Radyn cursed. She had heard him!

And chosen the gate instead.

A pit formed in Radyn's gut. If that was what she wanted, who was he to argue? He didn't know a thing about her except for the inhuman strength she possessed, and he couldn't help but think that such strength didn't belong in this world.

But she was so young.

He showed Tanwen what he intended. The dragon acknowledged the idea but didn't seem enthusiastic.

Radyn didn't blame him. Even if it defied all odds and worked, they were hurtling toward a surface that was rapidly swallowing the sky. It was probably already too late.

He shifted his feet, getting into a crouch so he could leap.

Kaya watched the shift in his posture and guessed at his madness. She glanced down at the surface, then tried to meet his gaze and shake her head.

The notes his spirit sang changed, swelling to a point where it was all Kaya heard.

His song was beautiful but unresolved.

If he jumped, that song would end along with hers.

Too early.

For the second time that week, Kaya put her trust in the Song, even though it wasn't the decision she would have made.

She closed herself off from the Song, surrendering it.

At least for now.

Tanwen felt the shift before Radyn did. He angled toward the falling girl. Radyn watched for a heartbeat, then returned to his sitting position. He helped guide Tanwen, and Kaya floated toward them.

They drifted closer and closer, Radyn always keeping

one eye on the rapidly approaching surface. Soon, she was close enough to reach out to, and Radyn did.

She reached for his hand, but it took them three tries. As soon as he had a firm grip, he pulled her closer. She got her legs awkwardly around Tanwen.

Radyn shouted, "Hold on!"

She wrapped her arms tight around his waist and he gave Tanwen the freedom to stop their descent.

The dragon spread its wings and expelled force from its spirit as quickly as it could. Radyn and Kaya were pressed against his neck, but he bled off speed and leveled out no more than fifty feet above the treetops.

Radyn took a deep breath and waited for his heart to stop pounding. After a few cycles of breath, he turned back to the girl.

"Name's Radyn. It's a pleasure to finally meet you."

21

Tanwen circled patiently above Starfall while Radyn studied the surface. It seemed too quiet. After everything Kaya had put the city through, he expected the surface to be flooded with survivors.

Then again, he well remembered what Aria was like after the fall of Whitehawk. Even though she'd been trapped inside a room for almost a full day, she'd been frightened of the surface for weeks after. She claimed it was easier to believe in the stability of the cities when one was enclosed within its hallways and rooms. Being on the surface reminded her they were a part of the sky and could fall at any moment.

Maybe it was the same here.

Or maybe the destruction was so widespread within the city no one had made it to the surface yet.

He saw two figures emerge from a stairwell. One walked smoothly, but the other favored one leg. They walked to where Radyn and Nikki had jumped off earlier.

Radyn advanced cautiously. He dropped below the

level of the surface while still well away from Starfall, then flew up so that no one on the surface would spot them. Tanwen landed softly in the field only a dozen feet from the fence.

Kaya slid off right away, but Radyn remained mounted while he searched for activity. The nest was on the other side of the city, and for a short window of time, the surface was mostly empty. No one had called out about Tanwen's arrival yet, though he imagined they'd be surprised to find the prints come morning.

Radyn also climbed off. Kaya remained close to Tanwen, using the dragon to shield her from Nikki and the older woman.

"What's wrong?" he asked.

Kaya pointed at the older woman. "She kidnapped me."

Radyn was about to protest but then realized he had no idea the suffering the girl had endured. He wouldn't trust anyone, either.

"She told me she wants to help you. I'm not sure I believe her, but if there's anyone who can explain what happened, it's her. I promise I'll protect you."

He'd expected more of an argument, so he was surprised when she nodded and traded Tanwen as her shield for him. The older woman grimaced as she got down on her knees and bowed deeply to Kaya.

"I'm sorry for everything, Kaya."

Radyn wasn't sure he believed her, but she was in no position to harm the young woman, so he kneeled across from her. Kaya did the same, behind and Radyn's right.

No one knew how to start the conversation, so Radyn

began. He looked over his shoulder to Kaya. "Perhaps we could start with you telling us how you got here and what happened to you once you arrived. Quickly, as I don't know how long we'll have."

Kaya did. She told them that she had traveled through the Engines, as naturally as one might say they'd gone out for a walk after supper. She recounted her adventures up until she'd stepped into Robyn's bedroom and discovered her friend murdered.

Miranda took over the story from there. She explained to Kaya how she'd been found and explained why they'd felt like they had little choice but to drug her again.

The storytelling took less time than Radyn would have expected. "I'd like for all of us to return to Firestone. Our Blade, Jyn, is eager to meet you," he told Kaya.

The young woman hesitated, but Radyn wasn't sure what other option she had. Starfall and Nightkeep were far too dangerous.

Miranda shook her head. "She can't return to Firestone. Her father's allies are there, too. As far as we know, they have allies in every city."

"In which case, Firestone is as safe a city as any for her. I can protect her, and I'm sure Jyn will, too."

"What if I told you there was another option?" Miranda asked.

Radyn frowned. "Besides a city? You want to send her to a colony?"

"I want to bring her to the surface with me and the people I represent," Miranda said.

"And that is?" Nikki asked.

"We call ourselves Soulkeepers. We've been working quietly through some of the smaller cities to set up livable habitats on the surface. We're still mostly underground, but we're learning. You would all be welcome, if you like."

Radyn shook his head. "I promised my Blade I would bring her to Firestone." He didn't add that if he failed in that, he was supposed to kill her. It wasn't a possibility he wanted to contemplate.

Miranda looked straight at him. "Do you believe that's wise? You've seen the reach of the group that includes Kaya's father. They count Singers, clan, and more among their allies. Do you believe that Firestone is somehow safe from their influence?"

"No, but I believe in my ability to protect her," Radyn said.

Miranda wasn't convinced. "I've heard your name whispered, Radyn. You're an outcast among your own people. Do you truly believe they'll allow you to protect her once they understand what she can do?"

She had a point, but Radyn wasn't yet swayed. He wasn't foolish enough to believe Firestone would be without danger, but Jyn was a competent Blade.

"Besides, how long do you think they'll let her live once they realize she's capable of controlling a city by herself? They'll see the possibilities, but after what happened tonight, they might not be willing to take the risk of having her within their precious city."

Radyn looked out at the devastated surface. He kept his thoughts away from the damage within the city. That was more pain and suffering than he wanted to endure. It wouldn't allow him to think straight.

He was still haunted by his memories of Whitehawk. And he'd promised Aria she'd never have to live through that again. Could he live with himself, knowing what he'd brought to Firestone? Could he live with himself, knowing he'd handed Kaya over to Jyn, who'd already made it clear that if he couldn't control her, he'd kill her?

Miranda had turned her gaze from Radyn to Kaya. "Besides, it's not your decision. It's hers."

Kaya stared firmly at the ground.

"I'll not force you to come with me," Miranda said, "but I believe you'll be happy with us. There are Engines on the surface, weak and flickering. We need someone who can bring them to life, someone who can teach them new tricks. We've been looking for someone just like you. Someone who can ensure humanity can return to the surface safely."

"Is it dangerous?" Kaya asked.

"At times, though we do what we can to stay safe. Some of us have lived largely on the surface for years, now."

Nikki stepped in. "Radyn, you can't let this happen. There are no Engines on the surface, and there's no humans, either. I don't know what she's planning, nor does it matter. The Blade's orders were clear."

"There are Engines on the surface. I've touched one myself," Radyn said.

"You have?" both Nikki and Miranda exclaimed at the same time.

Radyn nodded, though it was a matter for a

different time. The question now was what they did with Kaya. He turned once again to her. "What do you want?"

"Radyn—" Nikki warned him.

He ignored her and waited for Kaya to answer.

"I'd get to Sing to Engines by myself?" she asked Miranda.

"For as long as you want," Miranda assured her.

Kaya closed her eyes and Radyn felt her connect, not to shards, but to the Engine. Or maybe something deeper. It reminded him of Elora when she connected to the Engine at the end of her life. As he was still connected to Tanwen, it pressed against him like a physical force. Thankfully, the process only lasted a moment. Kaya opened her eyes, and Radyn was once again surprised by her certainty.

"I'd like to go with you," Kaya said, nodding to Miranda.

Miranda's relief would have been obvious to anyone. She bowed deeply in thanks, then turned to Radyn. "Will you take us? I had arranged transport, but I do not think anyone will be leaving the city soon."

Nikki spoke up again. "Radyn, if you take them, there will be hell to pay back in Firestone."

Radyn had been thinking just the same. Jyn would have him exiled if not outright executed. He'd be more forgiving if Radyn brought Kaya back, but if he caused all of this only to return empty-handed? It didn't take much to imagine the disaster.

On the other hand, he wasn't sure he wanted Kaya anywhere near Firestone. Not after what had happened here. And the girl wanted to follow Miranda down to the surface, which had to count for something.

He knelt between Nikki and Miranda, torn in two directions.

He stared hard at Kaya as though he might find answers in her face, and as he did, he felt as though he stared at a young Elora. It made the decision a simple one. He stood and brushed the dirt off his pants. He turned to Kaya. "If you want to go with her, let's go. I'll take you down before I return to Firestone."

Kaya stood cautiously, expecting a trap. When he didn't say anything else, a smile slowly grew on her face. Seeing her this happy made his future sacrifice worth it.

Nikki came close to him. "Radyn, you know what this will mean, right?"

He nodded. "Are you going to stop me? I'm happy to take all the blame, and I don't want to fight you."

She didn't consider for as long as he thought. "No. I won't."

Radyn took them all in with a glance. "Then we should get going before it's too late."

The flight away from the cities ended up being the most peaceful part of Radyn's day. After the chaos and uncertainty of the past hours, all four of Tanwen's passengers seemed eager to enjoy the ride in silence.

Nikki and Kaya looked as though they might have been twins. Both stared wide-eyed at the world passing below, enormous grins plastered constantly on their faces. Miranda, in contrast, looked as tired as Radyn felt, and more than once, he worried that she would fall off Tanwen as their journey progressed.

For his part, Radyn fretted about the future. He believed that what he did was right, but that didn't mean his actions would be devoid of consequences. If anything, life had taught him that he usually suffered the most for his greatest deeds.

Miranda guided them well, and Radyn never had to ask Tanwen to circle or backtrack. They passed over the prairie, which was the land most often found beneath Firestone, into an area of rolling hills. Off in the distance, the hills grew in elevation, providing a vantage point that would allow one to look out for miles. Eventually, Miranda pointed down, and Radyn followed her finger. They landed on a mound of a similar size and shape to one Radyn had explored many months ago.

The signs of recent human habitation were everywhere: well-worn paths, too thick to be made by any animal, crisscrossed the mound. Stone walls that came up to the height of his shoulders fenced off small plots of land that were currently barren but appeared to have been recently harvested. Radyn saw no cattle or pigs, but he wouldn't have been surprised to find them tucked somewhere more easily defensible. From where he stood, he could look up at the hills that had seemed so small from the sky but seemed much more imposing when seen from the ground. He was seized by a sudden urge to climb to the top and look around, but he shook his head. Some other day, perhaps.

Radyn expected a larger greeting party, but no one

came to greet them. Miranda bowed deeply to both Nicky and Radyn, then started hobbling down the mound. If it was anything like the one Radyn had visited, he expected there would be an entrance near the bottom.

Kaya matched the bow. Nervousness and excitement warred for control of her face, but it looked like excitement was slowly winning out.

Radyn bowed his head toward her. "I will come to check on you if I can, but I expect that you'll do well."

"Thank you for everything," she said. It looked like there was more she wanted to say, but in the end, she simply bowed again and ran off to follow Miranda, a slight skip in her step.

"Do you think it was worth it?" Nikki asked.

Radyn watched as Kaya offered her arm to help support Miranda. She seemed taller somehow, as though she'd grown just on the flight over. He smiled.

"Yes, I think it was."

22

———————

Radyn and Aria hadn't yet finished packing when the heavy knock sounded on his door. Radyn's gaze met Aria's, and with his eyes, he indicated that she should finish packing quietly. It had been a risk to come here and implicate her, but he had felt the risk justified. Radyn went to open the door, and as he expected, Jyn was on the other side. A storm brewed on the Blade's face, and Radyn was reminded that he wasn't sure if it came to a fight that he would win. He opened the door wider and gestured for Jyn to come in.

"Please close the door," Jyn said.

Radyn did. "Care for a seat?"

Jyn shook his head. He glared at Radyn, no doubt envisioning no small number of unique and creative tortures. Once he had satisfied his imagination's bloodthirst, his fists relaxed. "You must be the most stubborn and disobedient Sword that I have ever known. Give me one good reason why I shouldn't strike you down right now."

Radyn shrugged. "I believed it was the right thing to do."

Jyn thrust his pinky finger into his ear and pretended to dig wax out of it. "Is that all?"

"Anything else would be a lie."

Jyn's fists clenched again, and he paced through their small room like a caged animal. "I don't know how it's possible to have so much respect and so much frustration for the same person."

"If Elora was here, I am sure that you two could compare notes."

The comment slowed Jyn's steps until he came to a stop. "Why? Why did you do this? She could have changed everything!"

"Because after what she did to Starfall, I didn't want her anywhere near Firestone. Because the people who were after her sent a shiver down my spine and were willing to kill anyone to have their way, and I don't trust everyone in the clan. But most of all, because I think she hears something in the Song of the Engine that no one else does, and she uses that to guide her path. I know it's a foolish thing to say about a young girl who I don't know at all, but I trust her as much as I trust you, which is to say, completely."

"That was low," said Jyn.

"So is always getting me to do the work too dirty for you to touch. But I speak true."

"I can't protect you after this. In Starfall, dozens are dead and hundreds injured. What they endured makes our Little Fall look like nothing. Starfall has dragons, Swords, and Daggers dead, and one of their Singers has gone missing. Bridges are destroyed, most likely twisted beyond repair. It's a small wonder no one has yet declared war. I think the only reason no one has is because there hasn't been time to figure it out. But they will, and regardless of your intent or reasons, they'll find you at the center of everything. They won't settle for sending you to a prison colony."

"Then why haven't you arrested me?" Radyn asked.

"Because I can't decide if you've saved Firestone again or doomed it for good."

Aria came out of the bedroom. "You know the answer to that."

Jyn offered her a quick bow of his head. "I suppose I do." He shifted so he could glance behind Aria into the bedroom. He saw the packs on the bed and sighed.

"Tanwen?" the Blade asked.

"Sorry to leave you short a dragon."

Jyn waved his hand as if it was nothing. "Not like he's been doing much except eating and sleeping for us lately. Macken will be disappointed, but in the spring, there will be a new breed of younglings to pay attention to."

"Where will you go?" Jyn asked.

"To join the Soulkeepers. They need help protecting the land they're trying to build. I think Tanwen and I will really be able to help them, and Aria's crafting will be just as useful."

Jyn nodded. "Suits you better than being a farmer. That much is for sure."

"I think you're right."

Jyn bowed to them both. "Best get out quick.

Nightkeep wants extra dragon patrols in the sky as soon as possible. You'll want to be away before daybreak."

Jyn reached into a pocket and handed Radyn a letter. "This will help you with Macken."

Radyn smirked. "You knew what I would do."

"You're not the only one in this city with some wits. Though I'll admit, I wish there was a world in which you could have been my advisor."

Radyn bowed. "I feel the same. Before I leave, I should let you know I promised I would try to convince you to tell Nikki what happened during Nightkeep's attack. She's close to guessing, I think."

Jyn shook his head. "Be that as it may, with you and Aria gone, the secret is well and truly safe. She can keep guessing."

Jyn turned to leave. "Take care, Radyn."

"You too, Jyn."

The door closed behind the Blade and Radyn waited some time before opening the door again. Jyn wouldn't want them seen anywhere close together. Radyn held Aria's hand as they walked through the hallways.

"Are you sure about this? With me gone, the city would be yours to conquer as you please. You could have your pick of eligible men," he said.

"It wouldn't mean much without you. Besides, after tonight, I get a little sick thinking about being in the cities. I think it's time to try the surface. They'll need what I can build."

Radyn agreed. They took the steps two at a time and reached the surface. Radyn didn't take them toward the nest, though. He called to Tanwen as he stood in the field, he'd worked so hard in this past year.

"Why not the nest?" Aria asked.

"This way there's absolutely nothing to link Jyn to my escape. I trust Macken, but there's no reason to spread this wider than it needs to be. It also wouldn't surprise me if there were other clan up and preparing the dragons for the busy day ahead."

Tanwen arrived before long, and Radyn spoke to him. "Your days of leisure are at an end, friend."

Through their connection, Radyn felt Tanwen's pleasure at the statement. He wanted to hunt and fly.

Radyn climbed onto Tanwen, followed by Aria. He took one last look at the field that had been his. A field he and his father had worked when he was younger. He offered it a bow, then told Tanwen to take them back to the Soulkeepers.

Tanwen spread his wings and thrust himself into the air, and before long, Radyn and Aria were flying in the direction of the breaking dawn.

THE ADVENTURES CONTINUE!

Top of the morning!

I hope that wherever you are in the world, this finds you doing well. Thanks for reading, and I hope you enjoyed the story. In an age of endless entertainment options, the choice to spend your time in these pages means the world to me.

Night of Sword and Shield was an absolute pleasure to write, and I'm excited to share more of Radyn's journey and his world with you. Look for book 3 to arrive in August 2024!

Ryan

April 2024

ALSO BY RYAN KIRK
FIND THEM ALL AT RYANKIRKAUTHOR.COM

Saga of the Broken Gods

Band of Broken Gods

Fall of Forgotten Gods

Rise of the Resurrected God

Last Sword in the West

Last Sword in the West

Eyes of the Hidden World

A Sword Named Vengeance

Wraith's Revenge

Frontier's End

Song of the Sagani

Oblivion's Gate

The Gate Beyond Oblivion

The Gates of Memory

The Gate to Redemption

Relentless

Relentless Souls

Heart of Defiance

Their Spirit Unbroken

The Nightblade Series

Nightblade

World's Edge

The Wind and the Void

Blades of the Fallen

Nightblade's Vengeance

Nightblade's Honor

Nightblade's End

Standalone Novels

Blades of Shadow

The Last Fang of God

The Primal Series

Primal Dawn

Primal Darkness

Primal Destiny

ABOUT THE AUTHOR

Ryan Kirk is the award-winning and internationally bestselling author of over thirty fantasy novels spanning nearly a dozen worlds. He lives in Minnesota with his family, where he enjoys long, meandering walks outside even when the snow is high enough to cover his legs. When he isn't glued to his keyboard, he's usually in the woods, either on foot or on a bike.

RyanKirkAuthor.com
contact@waterstonemedia.net

 facebook.com/waterstonemedia
 x.com/waterstonebooks
 instagram.com/waterstonebooks